We are all a little Weird and life's a little Weird,

And when we find someone whose Weirdness

Is compatible with ours, we join up with them

In fall in mutual Weirdness and call it

LOVE

~Dr. Seuss~

~To all the Weird couples in Love, this book's for you~

Mayra Salazar, Cover~ Color Design

Eneyda Prado, Cat~Art Design

~Proofreaders~

Erica Caballero

Julie Squires

Vanessa Cantu

The Librarian Who Knew Too Much

By Enez Ensenia

Chapter One

In the small town of Catswillow, Melva contemplated on what to wear for her first day at the county library.

"Brinks," she turned to the handsome male sprawled out on her bed. "Do you think this is way too much, after all it is *only* the library?" Her voice cracked with emotion.

Her male didn't answer, just merely stared into space. She knew males didn't care what females wore, just as long it showed a little skin. Not that her male cared anything about the latter, to him it was all the same, as long as she catered to his every whim, he was content.

She placed a cranberry-colored dress against her body that without a doubt – exposed too much leg. She wanted to look nice, but didn't want patrons' thinking she was a harlot. Typical stereotyping of what a librarian or someone working in a library should look like – for example – wear stockings, (bare, pale legs a no-no), dowdy all the way, and don't forget eyewear that lets one peer out over the top of the lens. She was none of these things, but she thought she'd fit in nonetheless. She glanced at her male once more.

Brinks lay still as a statue, oblivious to the noise coming from the female with the worst taste in clothes, in his opinion; not that he knew anything about clothes, but if he were going to wrap something around his luscious body, it would be warm and made out of the finest cotton/wool blend. He would *love* that! He knew the 'getting place' for such a particular sweater he could wrap himself up in — what a yummy feeling...

Melva Klick, spinster and in this small town, many found her to be a little weird, even for a spinster. This wasn't her fault, after watching her mother and father do the most peculiar things with their pantry: alphabetizing the canned food, making sure everything labeled faced the front, coffee cups in the cupboard labeled on the bottom for every day out of the week, those sorts of things. Melva was a creature of her environment. She went around picking lint off her clothing, and off complete strangers who waited in line at the supermarket or the local coffeehouse. Most of the women

ound this habit … offensive, to say the least. The men, well they just thought she was
flirting with them. This was not an attempt to pick up men. She was just trying to help
others – in her view – to look their best.

She stood before her spotless mirror and really didn't like what she saw staring
back at her. Her hair was out of place. *Oh no, what's this?* It was a tiny piece of yarn
that started to unravel and peeked out of the sweater she was trying on. Not another
person would have noticed, but Melva did. She panicked.

"It's my first day at the Library and nothing to wear, and I'm going to be late, and
…"

Brinks meowed at Melva's annoying voice — he wanted some quietness while he
sniffed out that favorite sweater of his. Her number one male was annoyed with her. The
CAT – like all the other male species – wanted to seek out his "cave." Brinks jumped off
the luxurious bed and sashayed across the room to sniff out the closet.

The closet was Brinks' cave, but Melva knew all men had one, a place to hide and
avoid the noising female with whom they lived. A place they insisted to think and sort
things out for themselves. Yeah…right.

This was her first day as the Assistant Librarian. She had an MLS, a Master of
Library Science, which made her a real librarian, but this was a job and she needed one.
Besides, it was better than what was out there in the small town … nothing. And, she had
to act perfect and look perfect, or else the whole day was ruined and her career tossed out
the window.

She continued fidgeting and tugging at her clothes, one wrinkle and the world
would most likely end. "What if I say the wrong thing to a patron, or stamp the wrong
date. Surely Mrs. Lomechick would roll the correct date on the stamper." She winced at
the horrible thought and Mrs. Lomechick.

Mrs. Lomechick, the epitome of what a librarian acted and looked like. When she
interviewed her for the assistant job, she found it very rude for this woman to try to
straighten her desk, and ask if she'd like it dusted off.

When she applied for the position, she noticed just how dirty the windows were,
and asked Mrs. Lomechick if someone would clean them before her hire date.

Lomechick just sneered and said, "Perhaps you would like to clean them?" She
got up and stalked toward the circulation, gesturing Melva to follow her. She turned and

spoke to Melva, "you're hired and don't be late, I do not tolerate such ghastly behavior in my library!" Mrs. Lomechick said sternly. But, what she thought was: *You, my dear strange woman, are in need of psychiatric help. And why would I hire you? Because I need a life outside this hellhole called a library!*

The interview lasted all but ten minutes.

Off to a great start. Melva sighed as she left the library, feeling Mrs. Lomechick's frustration.

She sat down on the bed draped in expensive Egyptian bedding that her wealthy Aunt Bertha had sent her. Aunt Bertha, who – at the moment – was touring Europe with her fifth husband's money, God rest his soul.

Everyone knew her Aunt Bertha. Lord only knew how she managed to acquire such wealthy (gullible) husbands, but she did, and did it well. Bertha often boasted to anyone in earshot, "I'm richer than God!" All the while sporting her latest fashion faux pas, (her favorite ensemble consisted of an orange fur-lined dress that was about two sizes too small), she honestly thought going to the local market was same as going to tea with the Queen of England.

She was referred to as 'Banking Bertha' because she banked the money of the men she out lived and most folks around the small town just shrugged Bertha off as having a stroke of good luck. She had mysteriously outlived husband number three, a man in his mid-thirties (fifteen years her junior). Most figured he had an underlying health problem and left it at that. Bertha never elaborated to anyone about his sudden death, only that he was a severely depressed person. One day he thought best to drive his Maseratti off a cliff, leaving Bertha with millions to do as she liked and she liked giving to charity. Her favorite was, of course, her only niece, Melva. She also loved spending time in her mansion, just outside of London, that he left her.

Melva began to sniffle, she was so frustrated, exhausted, while still trying on clothes and feeling complete panic-stricken with thoughts of doom. She decided her best course of action was to stay in and think about what steps she could take to make things go perfectly tomorrow.

But wait, Lomechick will fire me if I'm late. That old goat would do such a terrible thing.

Her stomach in knots, she decided maybe another cup of coffee would calm her down. She got up and straightened the comforter, and walked to the kitchen. There was a pot full of Starbuck's coffee, but it had been sitting there for at least thirty minutes, and this was excessively long for it to be 'fresh.' She grounded up some more beans and the smell in itself calmed her down considerably. She looked around her kitchen to see what she could clean, or straighten a bit more; she found a hard water spot near the faucet knob and eagerly cleaned it. She felt so much better.

Good, all is spotless, but for whom? She thought about that for a second, not feeling the least bit ridiculous. *If robbers broke in, they'd be impressed with such a clean place, and would not make a mess.*

She looked up while pouring her fresh brewed Starbucks and noticed her furry 'son' balanced on one of her barstools waiting for any kind of morsel. (When hunger strikes a male — any male — hiding in his cave can wait!)

"You've eaten Cat, so no more. Really, you need to watch that ample butt of yours or you won't be able to fit in your litter box," she giggled and snorted.

Brinks stared at her as if to say, "You're stupid. You are beneath me. Feed me, damn-it."

To the cat, this wasn't the least bit funny. He turned so that he revealed his ever-so- lovely bottom.

"Guess you're mad now. Oh well, I have issues that are more important at hand than your one-eyed monster staring back at me." Brinks never looked back. The guilt trip set in. "Brinks, come back, I didn't mean it."

Fighting with her cat proved one thing … she really could use more friends who are human.

Melva's one good friend, Gerdy Drake lived in a condo, a few doors down from her. The complex was center of the small town where everyone knew you and your family.

Gerdy was messy and carefree and I don't give-a-damn attitude. She was a genuinely happy person who readily put up with Melva's constant cleaning, nit picking and worrying about catching some incurable disease from public toilet seats. Gerdy came from a long line of females who could handle anything. Gerdy's mom had a friend like Melva back in the fifties, and they're still friends. Gerdy hoped for that same everlasting friendship for her and Melva. Melva entered Gerdy's life quite suddenly and dramatically.

They were in the fourth grade, and in Catswillow just about everyone had a horse or two. Every day Melva walked past a horse farm, on the way to school, and stopped by to pet one of her favorite horses. Other kids began to notice her detour and soon they started stopping by to pet the horse. Melva became jealous when she saw others playing with him on a warm sunny day.

She got upset, ran up to the horse, and grabbed his head, "He's my friend, not yours!"
All the kids just laughed at her, including Gerdy.

Mr. Horse didn't like all the teasing and yelling, so he grabbed the skin off the back from the nearest pest, who was Melva, and bit right in. Horrified, Gerdy tapped the horse's large head and freed Melva from the Jaws of Horse.

Gerdy loved Melva, but she'd rather get a kick out of making Melva's life miserable, too. Just before Melva would pop over for a chat, she'd make a complete pigsty of her apartment. She found sheer joy in watching Melva's face wrinkle up, and squirm on the sofa because of candy wrappers with half-eaten chews, and magazines thrown about as if a burglar on a sugar high ransacked the place. Melva had no clue; she just figured Gerdy was a slob. She was right.

Melva poured herself a fresh cup of joe and peeked around the kitchen once more to make sure all was in its place, then wiped off the counter where the coffee pot sat. She glanced up at the clock and noticed she'd be late if she lollygagged around her apartment all morning. She really wanted this job and looked forward to meeting different people.

She decided she'd face the new day with a positive attitude — Starbucks did the trick every time.

She was sitting on her luxurious bed – deep in thought – stroking Brink's long fur, who decided to grace her with his presence. She was in eternal bliss – to be with ones cat - then the phone rang.

"Girl, are you dead or what?" Gerdy giggled and knew she was on her bed with that cat contemplating what to do next: clean or go to her new job.

"Oh, hi Gerdy, I was getting ready for work." She held the receiver away from her ear as if it were a cockroach. Gerdy didn't know what it meant to speak in a normal tone of voice.

"Liar! What you *are* doing is petting that damn cat and he doesn't even pet ya back, what a bummer. Are you ready yet? — If so, I'll drive ya today, whatcha say?"

"What I say, is no. I know that you're just making fun of me … I'll drive my car, thank-you-very-much."

"Oh, yeah, forgot about the Bentley or was it Mercedes?" Gerdy wasn't jealous — well, just a little.

"It's a Mercedes, Gerdy, and it's nothing to do with riding in *your* car, if that's what you're thinking." Melva cringed at the thought of all those candy wrappers on the floor attacking her, and the pebbles and rocks hitting her legs while Gerdy drove like a bat-out-of-hell with all the windows rolled down — no way! She would end up looking like Medusa when she got to work.

"Suit yourself girlfriend, but don't be late, it's so *not* cool, even for you, you weirdo." They were thirty-five, but Gerdy acted as if she were still in high school. Gerdy laughed aloud.

Melva asked, "Gerdy, how old are you like fifteen, or what?" She slammed the phone down before she heard Gerdy's smart-ass answer.

She dragged her butt up off the comfortable bed, Brinks in tow, and headed toward her walk-in closet full of 'nothing to wear.' She then noticed Brinks pulled off her most comfortable sweater from the hanger and then curled up on top of it, eyes closed shut in a matter of seconds. "You look so handsome when you're asleep." She cooed as she stroked her number one man.

Brinks peeked at her with one eye open and one eye closed. *Crazy woman leave me alone. Don't forget to leave food for me.* He licked his whiskers and drifted back to kitty dream world.

She decided to wear a long ankle-length skirt, black of course, with a soft angora tan sweater and a pair of Jimmy Choo boots from Aunt Bertha. The lint, of course, would bother her the whole day, as if she needed more of a challenge today. So, she slipped her Evercare pet hair roller into her oversized leather bag and felt more confident. After checking the stove three times, just in case Brinks learned to turn on the burners with his huge paws, or some force of nature decided to make a mess in the kitchen, she left her apartment.

She walked out to her private garage and noticed someone's fingerprint on the hood of the black and silver Mercedes.

"You would think people would not touch your car with their dirty hands!" She stomped her Jimmy Choo's on the pavement.
She unlocked her door, reached over, grabbed some napkins (for emergencies, and this was one), and began to clean the smudge finger print marks off. "There we go. Perfect."

Driving toward the county library, which used to be a courthouse, the car phone rang.

"Whatcha doing?" Gerdy asked, knowing Melva just left the condo parking lot.

"I'm on my way to work, so leave me alone, or I'll have a wreck then you'll *have* to take care of Brinks." Melva knew that Gerdy didn't really take to the feline-child of hers.

"Cool, I just wanted to see if you ever got out of the apartment. Was the stove off?" She waited for Melva to answer. Gerdy's day was going to be great if she could piss Melva off. It was already proving to be a great day.

"Actually it was and I only checked it once." She rolled her eyes behind her designer sunglasses.

"Liar. You know that I know you go 'round and 'round in that apartment just to see what's on or off. You have fun don't ya? Clearly you need to see someone about that."

"Gerdy, I'm not listening to you, you should be more supportive and you know how that devilish woman is, Mrs. Lomechick. I bet she already hates me." Gerdy spooked Melva into thinking Lomechick was a mean, wicked Librarian, mirroring the Wicked Witch of the West from The Wizard of Oz. Gerdy had that right.

Lomechick had taught Gerdy English back in middle school. Every now and again, you'd hear a kid in the back humming the wicked witches' theme from The Wizard of Oz. Somehow the theme song stuck, labeling Lomechick forever.

"Girl, just call me and I'll thrash her once for ya," Gerdy laughed and snorted.

"That's not going to happen, you told me she might be nice to me, since it's my first day and all, but she'll probably hate me anyway … Remember the interview, hello!? Oh great someone just pulled out in front of me and no light signal — what an ass!"

"I'll let ya go; come over to the coffeehouse if you can okay, bye."

Her stomach ached. *It must have been the three cups coffee. Maybe I will take Gerdy up on that offer, after all, it might just be what I need, a nice pick-me-up from my best friend — yeah right.* She decided to skip the coffee shop.

She headed toward the library's parking lot, and of course, all the close ones occupied by SUV's, what she liked to refer to, as *Big Fat Gorillas.* She would tell Gerdy, "You know the ones, they're the women on their cell phones cradling it with their head and shoulder; oblivious to all traffic surrounding them." Gerdy would just nod her head in agreement, Gerdy really didn't give a rat's ass, but she wanted to be supportive. Melva drove around to find the perfect spot, where no one would hit her new Mercedes.

The library was an old building built around 1800s or so, she knew she'd love working in an historical building. The upstairs part of the old courthouse was more or less just an area full of old books and miscellaneous rejects for which Lomechick obviously had no use.

Melva mused, "Maybe one day, Mrs. Lomechick would add that space to the library. It would make an awesome addition to the library, nice and big, and roomy. Right now, I bet it's just a cramped space full of spider webs and bugs."

Melva had no idea what creatures would be working with her, bugs were right up there along with lint.

Chapter Two

She walked into the library and noticed it was very busy for a Thursday morning. She wasn't quite sure why Lomechick hired her toward the end of the week, *"guess she had her illogical reasons."*

Lomechick was behind the counter fiddling around with the newspapers and magazines. She looked up and noticed Melva adjusting her skirt, sweater and hair.

"Miss Klick," the dragon-lady hissed. "I need you behind the desk at once," barked Lomechick and disappeared into her dragon's den.

"Yes ma'am I'm coming," she answered while still adjusting her outfit. "How are you this fine morning?" she asked through the windowed wall of Lomechick's office.

Lomechick glared at the wall. "Fine," she mouthed.

She turned toward the desk and clicked her Jimmy Choo heels, "There's no place like home, there's no place like home…" She was a true fan of *Dorothy's* famous wish especially at this very moment.

A large plump man threw down his books to check out. "I'm in a big hurry lady — late for an appointment." He tossed his card to her as if she were an animal expecting her to chow down on it ravenously.

Melva was horrified. *Idiot. Am I supposed to jump when you say 'jump?' I think not!* She checked him out quickly; the faster he was out of the library the better. "Jerk," she fumed.

By the time she knew it, a long line had formed. She glanced back toward Lomechick's windowed office, but to no avail, she just ignored her.

Patrons were so impatient this morning; she could hear the huffing and puffing. *They must all be related to Lomechick. Damn dragons. I only have two hands people!* She was exhausted in the few minutes she was there, on her first day at that. She knew her lipstick needed checking after the nervous licking she had done on her lips. She decided it was time for a restroom break. She went to Lomechick's office.

"Mrs. Lomechick, would you mind terribly if I went to the restroom?" She nervously played with the end of her sweater like a child sucking his thumb and fiddling with the security blanket. Yes, she felt pathetic.

The old crow just hissed something or another. A "yes" finally came out of her bird-like mouth.

Melva got to the restroom, which was on the top floor with all the old books and opened the squeaky door. "Oh, gross!" She noticed how awful the restroom was and it smelled like a portable potty out in hundred-degree weather. She fought back the urge to yak right there on the floor, and proceeded to lift up her skirt very gingerly to take her pee … when a giant black spider made a dash back behind the toilet.

"Oh, no, please not a spider! Shit!" She took some paper towels and was on a mission to find the creepy thing and flush it, if she could catch it in the next few minutes. If she didn't hurry it up, she wouldn't have time to primp and adjust things. *The damn thing needs to find Lomechick, crawl up in her desk and leave me alone.*

After about five minutes, Lomechick came banging at the door.

"Miss Klick you have twenty patrons waiting for you. Do you hear me? Hurry along."

"Coming, I'll be right there…" She placed toilet paper on the toilet seat so she could sit down without catching the germs the seat most likely owned. Next thing she knew part of her skirt was now in the toilet. "Oh, double shit!" She panicked. Now she was sweating. "Now, that's attractive." Balancing herself with one hand on the wall, knees bent (she'd learned the awesome technique of balancing from Star Dusting, the Yoga teacher, from classes her and Gerdy took last summer) and Choo's firmly on the ground, she was able to go. Then she proceeded to wring and wipe her skirt off. She wanted to die. But, she had to get back to work, dreading the sneers and looks. She proudly walked down the steep stairs with a skirt trailing behind her, sopping with toilet water.

Her first day was a complete disaster; "*What more could go wrong?*" she wondered.

"Miss, you got anything for STD's?" A bald stout man asked loud enough, even demons from hell could hear him.

Melva was horrified. "Well, personally no — but have you checked the disease section? Hold on, I'll be right with you." *Could this stupid man be any louder? Idiot.* She grunted. She placed her pen down, walked over to show the man where to find his "subject" and came back to the desk.

When she got back, the circulation desk was a mess. *Must have been the old crow Lomechick. That woman must live in a pigsty.* Melva couldn't stand it; she immediately started putting things in their place, and made the desk presentable.

"Hi there uh…" a plastic-faced woman came up to the desk with her brood and read her nametag.

"Uh, Melva, is that it?" Her smile resembled that horse that bit Melva years ago.

Clear as day lady. What the hell do you want? I think I have to pee again, crap.

"How can I help you?" She put on a fake smile.

"Yes, me and my little angels here…aren't they cute?"

Hell no, they're evil trolls!

She swore she was having a major PMS attack. *I could use some chocolate right now.*

The crazy woman continued, "We'd all like library cards today." The woman waited and smiled bearing her large horse-faced teeth.

"Well, I'll need to see proof of residency. Do you have that?" Her voice strong and firm, she didn't blink an eye.

"You don't have to be rude about it; and no I do not — my license, is at home," her smile faded, now she looked like an ugly horse.

"Ma'am, you have to have some proof as to where you live —

Horse-face hissed, "Let me talk to Mrs. Lomechick, *she* knows me."

She turned and motioned Lomechick to come to the desk.

"What's the problem now, Melva?" She glared at her through her half-moon glasses.

"This woman here says you know her, she wants a library card."

"Well, give it to her!" Lomechick snapped.

"She doesn't have proof of residency." She was now very irritated with both 'animals.'

"Mrs. Lovecharm, do you have your check book or car insurance with you?" The woman pulled out her checkbook and glared at Melva. (She somehow remembered it was there all along).

What a total bitch.

"Of course I do, all she had to do was ask for it," the horrible woman triumphantly removed her documents. "See, all you have to do is ask for the information," the smart-assed woman replied.

"Okay, this will work. Melva will take care of you. Good day now." With that, Lomechick went back into her crow's nest.

The woman *and* her kids were annoying; the boys took after their mother, no doubt. They crawled all over the counter knocking things off left and right, and making a complete mess. All the while, the woman stood by cooing at her Children of the Corn.

She was exasperated, and when one of the brood dropped his filthy, slobbery sucker on her hand, and then sneezed in her face, she quickly slammed their materials on the desk and ran for dear life up to the restroom.

Lomechick just shook her head and sighed.

Once again, in the restroom, Melva contemplated whether this job was worth it. "I need to call Gerdy … I can't believe this is happening to me. Okay, calm down Melva," she spoke calmly into the dilapidated mirror.

"I'll go back down after I clean this off and start over, but first I'll call Gerdy. She'll tell me what I should do. Maybe I'll go work for her, that'll show Lomechick, I don't need this stupid job."

Lomechick banged on the door. "Are you going to stay in there all day? I do not pay for restroom visits. I expect you to return at once to your workspace. Melva, are you in there?" Lomechick huffed like a big bad wolf and stormed off.

She was clearly having a panic attack, "My sweater is filthy, my skirt is dirty, and my make-up is smudged, my God I can't do it … I can't!" She told her reflection. She sat on the filthy commode and put her face in her hands … *now for sure my make up looks like crap.*

With her hands shaking, she tried her best to wipe the contents of her soiled outfit properly clean. No luck, her outfit was now worse off than before. "Someone kill me now," she sulked and sat on the toilet again. Her Jimmy Choo's had a new scuffmark so she wiped that clean too, feeling a bit better.

Finally, she made it back down to the circulation desk where a number of superfluous patrons stood anxiously and impatiently for her.

"Who's next please?" She sulked in plain sight. *I want my kitty.*

Her cell phone rang in the tone of the The Pink Panther. She looked adoringly down at it and wished she could take it and throw it at the next patron. But this would only make matters worse no doubt. She leaned over to see who was calling her and it was Gerdy, she really wanted to answer it.

But Lomechick was eyeing her disgustingly behind her half-moon glasses, licking the front of her teeth copiously.

She continued to work and help patrons, and figured she'd get a break, but to no avail, a woman carrying two large medical books waltzed up to the desk.

"Hi there!" The patron sang happily. She smelled of mothballs, poor thing.

She looked at her with exhaustion, "Yes ma'am what can I do for you?" Her shoulders slumped.

"I was wondering what you suggest I get for irritations of the skin, or things like funguses … have any clue? I seemed to have found this book and this one." She placed each book on the counter for her to choose.

"Well, what is it that you are exactly looking to solve, a skin—?"
The woman interrupted.

"Oh, no, no … look here." She began to lift her blouse off her shoulder to expose a grossly round ulcer or some kind of ailment.

She held her hands to her mouth. She murmured to the woman, "Uh, ma'am maybe you should go see a doctor for that. I don't know what to tell you, just take both books — I'll need your library card at once." Melva checked her out, and stood back as far as she could without dropping anything on the floor while handing the materials to the patron.

The two other patrons behind her were also nauseated by the affliction. Who wanted to see that and right before lunch. Melva quickly got the woman and the others checked out and out the door.

She picked up her phone while Lomechick wasn't spying on her with her piercing eyes, and called Gerdy.

"Java Jar, Gerdy here, what can I do ya for?"

"Gerdy, are you supposed to answer that phone like that?" She felt like picking on Gerdy.

"Like what?" Gerdy spoke to some caffeine-hungry junkies while juggling the phone. "What's up Melva, are you home already? Hey, why didn't you answer earlier?"

Melva sighed heavily through her phone.

"No stupid, I'm still here … I've been a little busy," she began to sniffle, "I'm just miserable, no one likes me and there are 'things' all over the place, dirty things."

"Good gosh Melva pull yourself together, you really need to get laid — is that buzzard Lomechick giving ya a hard time already?"

She composed herself and ducked further behind the desk. She felt like disappearing and then rematerializing in her condo.

"No, nothing like that — well, she is a bit much for the first day, but no … it's not just her — like I said it's so gross in here and it smells." She just knew Gerdy wouldn't be helpful but held her breath anyway.

"Is anyone there that can hear how paranoid and stupid you sound, you know you won't catch any kind of incurable diseases there, or do ya think?" Gerdy laughed a hearty laugh.

She was oblivious to Gerdy's insensitive comment.

"What time can you do lunch? Can I come over there?" Melva needed her caffeine fix.

"Well, promise you won't try to clean up the place."

"Gerdy, thanks you're a great friend, even though I know you're being despicable toward me. See you around noonish, ok, bye!" Melva hung up the phone, preceded toward the animal section to shelve books.

Chapter Three

Melva anxiously waited for the noon hour so she could flee from the bug infested old library. She was dreaming of the Grande café mocha. When in walked the most gorgeous man she had ever seen. He was immaculate, every inch of him and she thought she just might be in love. *"In your dreams, girl,"* she told herself.

He looked around, and from the look of things, he wasn't impressed, (she didn't blame him), he took out a white handkerchief and wiped his hands. Her eyes opened wider. "My kind of man," she clasped her hands together in excitement. *He's a clean man, I can tell...*

She sighed and looked at this tall drink-of-water with lovingly eyes. She reached down for her purse while not taking her eyes off him. He was so perfect. Hard to find a man around her condo complex who bathed at least twice a week, so this was a real treat.

She nervously stood in what she called her 'sexy pose' and waited for her future husband to say something. Nothing wrong in dreaming a little at work, she figured.

"Hello," the stranger purred like Dracula. Melva had a thing for Dracula. She thought he was the most romantic, her favorite being Mr. Christopher Lee, of course.

She cleared her dry throat as she approached him. "Are you looking for a particular book?" She tried to coo professionally.

"Nah, just need your microfilm room please, meeting someone, and I need to look up an old newspaper."

He smelled so good, good enough for her to eat. She wanted to dive right in and smell his hair.

She fumbled along the desk and proceeded to meet the man around the corner to show him where to go. Her Jimmy Choo's caught a small indent from the old worn out carpet; she tripped and landed right in the stranger's arms.

He began kissing her hungrily and ravished her body with a spirit of a hungry beast. While all the patrons watched in awe.

She had hoped this had happened, but he simply stood her back up against the wall.

"Are you all right, Miss?" He purred again, ready for his bite.

She regained her composure and pointed out an empty spot next to another man.

"You can take that seat. I'll get someone to unlock the microfilm room." She sped off back toward the circulation desk. *I wonder if he's looking at me.* On her way to get Mrs. Lomechick to unlock the door, she looked back at him and smiled, and tripped again, this time into the arms of a man merely wanting to check out a magazine.

She couldn't keep her eyes off the stranger; he was so mysterious. His hair was as dark as the night with a touch of gray here and there. He reminded her of a character right out of one of her favorite racy-vampire novels by Amanda Ashley she loved to read the ones Gerdy refers to as "porno" in writing … Her thoughts interrupted by the library's phone.

"Hello, public library." She turned her back to the men in the chairs.

"What the hell are you still doing there? Get your ass over here!"

"Who — is this?"

"It's Gerdy, ya comin' or not?"

"Oh, yeah! Boy do I have someone to tell you about, he's simply dreamy. Wait for me okay?"

"Where the hell would I go? Melva I work all damn day!" Gerdy slammed the phone down and cursed again, silently in the back of the coffee shop where the private phones stood.

Gerdy's boss, Earl came around the corner. "Girl, got some customers out there, hungry like wolves for their coffee, best get out there. I gotta take a whiz, be right back." Earl owned two coffee houses. By first glace he resembled a cook in a greasy spoon. Looks were deceiving; he was a great businessperson, and had people skills to brag about, but he hated Melva.

She high-tailed it right over to the Java Jar in hopes of being welcomed by that Grande café mocha.

The Java Jar was two blocks away, but by Melva's gasping for air, it could have been two miles. As soon as she opened the door to the coffee shop the whiff of the variety of beans took her beyond blitz; a man would have brought her this same euphoria, but there was no man for her, just coffee for now.

Gerdy waved her down.

"Same? Or do ya wanna try something else today?" she asked knowing damn-well Melva was 'stuck in a rut of mochas.'

"I'll have the same. But make it really hot, last time it was lukewarm and you now I hate cold coffee," she scanned the room for the best clean spot to enjoy her mocha. Last time she was in, she tried to arrange the sugar and saltshakers, and then refilled the napkins dispensers. Earl caught her and cursed her out in front of a crowd of grungy kids, who just laughed at her. This was just one reason she despised Gerdy's dirty boss. Feelings between the two were mutual.

"Hey, where's the boss?" Melva asked, hoping to avoid her adversary.

"Oh, he's around, probably making another deal for another coffee place, why? Want me to fix ya up?" Gerdy giggled and spilled a little of the mocha mixture on the floor. She was relieved that Melva, caught up in herself to notice; otherwise, she'd fly behind the counter and start wiping down messes.

She was horrified. "Absolutely not, I've got better taste than that."

"Better taste than me? I doubt that, you are too old for me anyway…" Earl had overheard her rejection on his way back toward the front of the counter.

"Now, now, Earl uh, Melva was just going to sit for a while. A break for me too, okay?" Gerdy knew he was not the least bit offended by Melva's remarks.

He had a girlfriend who fit him to a tee. She also ran a few coffee places in upstate New York, and like him, she always looked as if she needed a weeklong soak in a tub.

"Really Gerdy, how can you stand to work here … and with him?" Melva wrinkled her nose as if she smelled stinky socks.

"Melva, not everyone has the luxury to work with the 'Bride of Frankenstein' like you do." Gerdy would take Earl over Lomechick anytime.

"Oh god, here he comes again, honestly doesn't he have anything better to do, like wash up, or something?" She wanted complete privacy in order to enlighten Gerdy of her new beau.

Earl continued to give her a monstrous glare while she stared back at Earl as if he were made of slime.

"Would ya stop lookin' at Earl that way? Geez, he might take offense."

"Well, he started it," she hissed mimicking a child.
Earl came over anyway.

"Hey Earl, my break's not over is it?" Gerdy hoped not.

"Nah, I wanna give this gal a piece of my special biscotti, hope ya like it sweet cheeks." He winked at her and threw down the plate, and strutted off exposing part of his crack, plumber style.

"I'm not eating that crap," she pushed the morsel toward Gerdy.

Gerdy ate the biscotti in two bites, not giving a crap about her weight. "Now get on with it I don't have much time, you seemed to have pissed him off, why else would he want to feed ya," Gerdy laughed.

"Okay, don't laugh at me, but I think I've met Prince Charming at the library, and you know he reminds me of one of those dreamy characters from the Dracula movies, with a little hint of gangster — and boy do your salt and pepper shakers need filling and cleaning — they are filthy!"

"Hold up. And can you for once stop reviewing all the 'uncleanness' around you? Who's a gangster?"

Gerdy's voice trailed around the small coffee shop, and the customers stopped sipping their drinks, suddenly interested in Melva's conversation.

She shockingly looked around. "No, dummy, he's not a mafia guy he just dresses like one," she whispered.

"Melva, you can't be serious … did he talk to you?"

"No, not a lot, he came in to look up stuff in the microfilm room. He was so handsome and clean, and if he comes back, I'm going to ask him out. I'm tired of everyone thinking I'm an old spinster in this town."

"You are," Gerdy spoke the dreaded truth.

"I am not and stop interrupting me …"

"All right, hurry though, this place is getting packed and I know Earl will scream for help soon."

"Well, as soon as he walked in I knew, that he knew, that I knew, that he liked me, isn't it wonderful?" Her hands clasped together and her eyes were as big as her coffee mug.

"What the hell did you just say?"

Melva started whispering again, "he knows that I know …"

"—forget it Melva, I can't listen to you anymore. When you start making sense call me — oh, hell no, don't call me I'll call you. I wish I could go home now; you've exhausted me with your stupid notions of some made up stupid guy." She threw her hands in the air and headed back behind the counter while the nosey customers looked on to see what Melva would do next.

She got up and waved at Gerdy, "see you later, you're coming to follow me home, so don't forget bye!" And trotted happily out the door.

"What a fruit cake," one of the customers snickered. Gerdy and Earl started laughing loudly, and got back to work.

On the way back to the library, Melva gazed up to the sky and hoped that her mysterious beau had not left yet. She wanted to strike up the nerve to ask him out, but not in front of old crow Mrs. Lomechick.

Mrs. Crow met her at the door.

"Where have you been? It's been way too long for a break, Klick?" The old librarian tapped her foot and waited for an answer, which she knew it would be a horrid excuse. Mrs. Lomechick thought Melva was horrid excuse for an assistant.

"Oh, yes, I was having coffee with my girlfriend Gerdy, oh she's a great gal, and you know her ..."

"I do not want to know any of your friends. Got that! Get back to work. By the way I expect you to stay rather late my dear Miss Klick to make up for this retched display of work you've done today — any questions, good, now back to work." The crow went back to her nest to nestle into her paper-filled desk.

Melva needed to wash her hands. She could do this and at the same time check to see if Mr. Right was still in the library. Lomechick had ruined everything when she walked in and attacked her for wrongly assuming she was late. This added to her nervousness. She had to find him, "it's now or never," she told herself as she tried to regain her confidence.

Melva looked around to make sure no one was watching. She bent over and tousled her hair with vigorous motions, then threw her head back emulating the models who used this maneuver to produce gorgeous hair effects. When she finished she noticed a couple of patrons staring at her from a distance waiting to see if the "Clairol Girl" would swish her hair from side to side. She turned red and waved to the onlookers, and proceeded to the microfilm room. When she got there, she noticed that great head of hair — she was so excited she could just spit!

She did the best catwalk (she learned this by watching Brinks) she could muster and when she got to the small desk, a man was sitting there, he appreciated the sexiness of it all, but he was not the mysterious stranger.

"Oh, hello there, do you need anything?" she smiled nervously.

"Uh, no, but thanks for the show I like the way you did that walk for me," the man stood up and headed toward the doorway. "I'll be back tomorrow if you do this for me again." He winked and left.

She felt heat on the back of her neck; it was Lomechick breathing heavily like a mad dragon.

"Are you quite done?" Lomechick with arms crossed and nostrils flared waited for her response.

"Yes, ma'am, I'll be right back, I have to ..."

"Miss Klick, do you want to keep your job?"

"Yes — yes of course I do."

"Your work is not in the restroom, where you've been running to all day."

Melva did want to wash up, but losing her job here on her first day would be tragic she couldn't bear the thought. She wanted Lomechick to like her — at any expense.

Lomechick piercing stare illuminated disgust.

"I'll get back to the circulation desk right away," Melva turned and slinked away another Brinks move. She knew she wanted a job at the library, but felt as if she stayed she couldn't be honest to Mrs. Lomechick, or to herself; she really needed some direction, but there was nobody to talk to here.

She didn't have to work at the library, but she truly loved the books and history of the building, and her aunt would be proud of her doing things for herself and not depending on anyone else for help. Yes, she wanted things perfect, no snags here or there. She thought about the gorgeous stranger. Would he judge her also? Maybe so, but this was something she had to face without reservations so that she could go forth and embark upon a happy, fulfilling life. She was entitled to this just like everyone else.

Melva took a deep breath and noticed by her watch it was fast approaching the evening hour; she so wanted to see her cat, she missed him terribly. *He must be hungry and totally lost without me,* she thought. She would be disappointed if she knew he wasn't the latter.

Lomechick left earlier to go home to her emus, two pigs, and a husband. Relieved to have the place to herself, Melva locked the doors to the front of the library and waited for Gerdy to meet her.

She could use a piece of chocolate, or something that melted on contact to the tongue, something that offered her stimulus effects. She dug in her organized purse, but to no avail, all she found was a slightly opened gum, but she thought better not, it might be stale, or have something on it. She sat down on the curb and chewed on her tongue instead, "oh Brinks I miss you," she glanced at her watch, "boy, your Auntie Gerdy is late."

Chapter Four

"Hey Paulie you gonna clean your piece all day?" Gino sat down at his Nonna's table and began eating some antipasti. "My nonna is the best, man, betcha she beats out your mamma's cookin' anytime." Gino's nonna, (grandmother), was a small Italian fireball – and in his opinion – the best cook imported from Italy.

Paulie continued to clean his gun, stroking it as if were a small kitten, "Ya know Gino instead of stuffing your big mouth, maybe you should be making plans to meet with Johnny "Big Bones." Johnny was a crewmember who took orders from the *capo*, who in this case, was Paulie's Uncle Frankie. "And find out when we need to leave this stinkin' town, Pussywillow." Paulie slid next to his pal and began stuffing his face.

"Hey, it ain't like that it's called Catswillow, get it right, man."

Paulie's face turned red, "Don't ya ever correct me, it's impolite, and I'm a guest here remember that. So, I'll call it anything I want."

Gino stuffed his face with some sauce and bread, "yeah, you can call yourself a guest here, but don't get smart, I'll smack ya next time, got that."

"You try it — go on — try it, I'll…"

"Abbastanza!" Gino's grandmother yelled and hit Gino upside the head and proceeded to pick up all the plates with piles of antipasti still on them.

"Sorry, Nonna," Gino sulked, "see, you've upset her and now she probably won't cook for you again, happy? Guess we'll have to eat later," he continued to sulk. He loved Nonna's cooking.

Paulie shrugged, "Guess I'll have that ditzy redhead I met today cook for me." He thought about how sexy she was even though she was a little weird for his taste.

Gino laughed boldly, "The one that was tripping and falling all over ya? She's a real fruitcake, you can tell. What the hell Paulie, ya hard up or something?"

Paulie ignored the comment. After the antipasti, he had a craving for a nice cigar. He hated this town. He couldn't believe it didn't have a place where you could buy nice cigars. All this town had were antique stores, cafés and a library. But the library, at least, seemed to offer him a nice quiet place to think is all.

His mamma hated the fact he was out here in the U.S.A. without her to cook, clean and cater to him; this was after all, how it was for him in Italy. Actually, all men living at home with mamma catered to their sons; it was the way of life there. He had big plans, his mamma didn't like it, but he followed example of his uncle. Still he missed his mamma.

Paulie had the utmost respect for Uncle Frankie and before long Paulie was in on everything that Uncle Frankie had plans on with his 'boss.' Even when Uncle Frankie took his *'Omerta,'* they instructed him to make himself invisible, but to listen with caution to the *'Omerta,'* because when he became a man, he too would take this oath. Violation to this code was inescapably, death.

Paulie's extraordinary talents and ideas made him *capo* early on; he was quite young, only twenty-six at that time. He was at the top of the ranks when a dispute progressed with a younger man wanting nothing to do with his instructions. Ultimately, the Organization sent instructions to him to make his way down to this small town to get some things started up here, with the don's approval.

The don didn't want any kind of problems with either young man that would result in one or both reprimanded. They both did great work for the don. Therefore, the don sent Paulie one place and the other person to another town far away from each other.

Paulie, sent here to Gino, his *consigliore*, (counselor), but this wouldn't stop him from taking control over what he thought was his turf.

Paulie had big plans, and no one was going stop him from succeeding at them, not even Gino. Today he came up with a plan to make that library into a place where he could do some business, and make some money of his own; he was smart he could do it. One way was to make that girl he saw help him, without her knowing it of course, (It shouldn't be a problem she seemed somewhat eager to help), and he frowned.

He decided to get Gino in on the action when the time was right, but he would have to make his move on the girl soon. Paulie didn't think that would be a problem, people always used the library every day. He'd have to find out her schedule, scope out her routine and find out whom she hung around. This would be interesting for him, he wasn't really attracted to her, but she'd do if it came to that. He grinned to himself at the thought.

He wasn't sure if Gino would participate in his plan, but he would talk to him about it later on over a meal, Gino was a sucker for good food. There was an Italian 'hole in the wall' over next to a coffee shop he noticed around town and not that far from the library. He decided to make Catswillow *his* town.

Gino had to make a phone call in private to The Boss Stallinoz, so he headed outside with his cell phone. He did not want to be disrespectful to his nonna and make the phone calls from her house. The less his nonna knew the better; the little Italian firecracker was no dummy. She knew more than she let on.

Paulie, on the other hand, decided he was fed up with sittin' around doin' nothin.' He had cleaned his gun enough, but looked forward to using it; maybe shoot some targets out in a field, anything from going nuts in the small town. "I'm going for a walk, Nonna. need to work off this pasta," he said patting his stomach. He bent over and kissed her on top of her head. *"What a feakin' drag having to tell the old lady where I'm going, stupid Gino and his stupid plans to stay here."* His bad mood was due to the lack of privacy and getting laid. He was so use to giving everyone orders to leave the Italy house when he needed his space and privacy.

He walked around to the corner store, grabbed a chocolate bar and coke, and headed toward the library on foot. It was about two miles from Nonna's house, but he'd get Gino to pick him up when he was done being nosey about the crazy girl that worked there. He was a handsome man, so it was a given that he'd turn all the women's heads when he passed them by along the sidewalk. A few of them even whistled. He knew he looked good, so he acknowledged one in particular and tapped her butt when she walked by. "Small town broads gotta love 'em." Something funny was happening to him though, when he'd see these other girls he'd start thinking of the girl in the library.

"Maybe she has some kind of voodoo on me," he concluded. He didn't want her, or so he thought. *"I just want to use her is all,"* he assured himself.

As Paulie turned the corner he noticed the library's parking lot was empty, "shit, it's closed," he huffed and proceeded to walk toward the steps. He stopped when he noticed the girl sitting on the steps of the old building, obviously talking to herself.

"What a whack job," he said under his breath. But, she seemed so sweet and innocent like someone that would take care of him, like his good mamma. "Aren't these the kind of women you're supposed to marry?" The thought quickly left his mind, she wouldn't know what to do with a man in his type of position, or would she? "Nah," he figured, "she's more of Gino's type, dumb." He hid and watched anyway, she was pretty animated and entertaining to him.

A car drove up, stopped and she went over to talk to that person.

"Gerdy you are late and you know Brinks could be starving, poor thing, geez ever think of him?" Melva lost it, "you know he loves his dinner and some kisses. What will I tell him if he doesn't get all this on time?"

"Melva, you know I could care less about what Brinks thinks, so do me a big favor get in and I'll drive you to your car so that I can toss you out on your ass!" Gerdy was in no mood for Melva's drama, it was late and she was hungry.

"Fine! But don't say I didn't warn you about him being upset next time he sees you." She reluctantly got in Gerdy's nasty car. Gerdy sped off like two bats out of hell.

Paulie watched the two broads and listened to every word. "Who the hell is Brinks?" Was he a boyfriend or worse, a husband? He did not want to have to 'whack' the dude, but he would if he got in his way. He only wanted to deal with her…excited also by this new, weird challenge.

A moment later, he saw the crazy broad driving back down the street. "Who would drive someone to their car that they could so easily walk to?" But, what interested him more was the car. "Nice Mercedes, Melva," he whispered.

Chapter Five

Melva made a mad dash into the condo where she was convinced poor Brinks must have been starving to death. "Honey, I'm home!" Her personal home security system had ransacked the condo: toilet paper was all over the living room, and one of Aunt Bertha's priceless vases was in tiny pieces on the floor. The undeniably culprit sashayed across the floor and slumped his ample rump on the ground, mirroring a man that had just put in a ten hour workday. She ran to the phone and called Gerdy, she wanted his "aunt" to feel the full wrath of her anger.

"Yeah, what's up?" Gerdy answered.

"Auntie Gerdy is in deep shit no doubt; you know what your nephew did since I was so late getting home?" She looked around and started calculating how long this would take her to clean up, and then a panic attack set in because she didn't have any more dusting cloths. "It's your entire fault, Gerdy, he could have been killed!"

"What the hell are you talking about?" She felt Gerdy's nonchalant attitude through the phone.

"There's glass all over the place, and he's acting funny, and I've got to clean this up now!" She screamed through the phone.

Gerdy sighed, "Is that all? He's probably wondering what he's going to eat. I swear that is all he does; he's a damn cat, Melva."

She was floored now. "He's not *just* a cat, he's my child and since you cannot bear to hear that then I'm hanging up on you now, good-bye," she waited to see if Gerdy would apologize ..., waited ..., and waited.

"Melva let's just go out to eat, it was your first day on the job and you just need to chill out a bit, okay, my treat."

Melva didn't really want to eat out, because she had so much to do by morning, but she was hungry. She knew she couldn't ask Gerdy to help her clean up the mess, because she'd have to clean up after Gerdy. She was exhausted thinking about this, but hunger won. "Okay then, but let me feed Brinks first and make sure he eats, so give me about an hour then come on over, I'll drive us."

Gerdy agreed and she decided to wait out the hour in a luxurious bath. She had to get ready for 'Melva night,' she'd relax now since her dinner companion would be stressing out over everything and anything.

Paulie, back at Nonna's place, found Gino in front of the TV laughing and clapping his hands while watching *The Price is Right* with his nonna. He rolled his eyes at Gino. Gino noticed Paulie's irritation and told his grandmother to leave the room; he had business to talk with Paulie. She stormed out of her living room and slammed her bedroom door after she made it clear she wasn't his slave, and then refused to cook for him in the future since he was so disrespectful toward her.

"Paulie, you're bad luck man, now my nonna won't cook for me anymore, what we gonna eat now?"

"Man, fuhgeddaboudit, you should worry more about making some money than eating your way outta your suits, let's go down to this place I saw on my way back here. It looks like a good place to have some pasta and a drink. Got a plan and I think it'll work."

"Does it include that broad?" Gino asked suspiciously.

"Yeah, so you wanna go or not?"

Gino looked around the empty place and shrugged, "Yeah, I could eat."

"And what else is new, my *Compagno*," they both laughed and patted each other on the shoulder and left.

Gerdy showed about an hour later holding a can of StarKist tuna for the guilty party; she figured this would give his 'mother' a sense of relief on getting him fed. Melva vowed that Gerdy was back to number two on Brinks list of favorite females. They left after Melva checked her stove for the fourth time.

Bella Rini was a quiet Italian place sandwiched in between two antique stores, it had a cozy European feel unusual for Catswillow. The waitress that met them at the door was indeed out to capture all the males' attention.

"It would have helped if she at least worn a bra…," Gerdy whispered to Melva after the vamp seated them.

The place was not that busy; so the one waitress was it for everyone. They sat at a table near the back patio. It was a lovely setting with its palm trees and tropical plants and flowers embedded near the narrow fence. If one wanted, they could go out on the spacious patio and enjoy all the aromas the gardens offered and eat their meal. The girls just wanted to eat and therefore decided the outdoors was too romantic for just the two of them.

Melva looked over the table and chairs, protested a bit about it being dirty so the waitress obliged her and gave the furniture a once over with her filthy rag.

"Don't make a scene; I swear I'll take you home right now!" Gerdy scolded. "We are going to relax and talk about the handsome devil you're supposed to go out with soon, remember that topic?"

"Yes, I remember, how could I forget he's absolutely gorgeous, but I have to pee first — I'll be right back, so do *not* order for me." She sped off toward the restroom.

The double D sized waitress appeared, "What can I get you gals tonight, some wine or just tea?"

"Oh, let's see," Gerdy debated in her mind quickly how much trouble she'd be in if she ordered everything right now. She was so hungry. She really didn't care if Melva got mad.

"Okay, let's see…I'll start with your house salad — make that two, one for me and one for her. Well, hell — I'm just going to order for us both, ready?"

The waitress had her pen ready, "Go ahead."

"I'll have your Chicken Marsala … and to drink, a merlot for now."

The waitress nodded her head at Melva's chair, "What would she like?"

Gerdy grinned, "Get her your house Pasta Primavera and a salad, and to drink…she likes those 'splits' you've got in the Rossi wine, okay?"

"Great, it'll be right out."

"Thanks." Gerdy hoped Melva wouldn't cause a scene when she got back to the table.

The waitress sped off to take another tables' order. Gerdy looked around and wondered what was taking Melva so long.

Melva was busy in the restroom making sure all was in its place: her outfit; her hair; her lipstick, and was trying to tidy up the place a bit from the last customer – "the slob."

The waitress brought Gerdy's drink just in time, she needed some alcohol and fast, this way she was numb a bit by the time dinner came. She looked up when she heard the tiny doorbell ring and noticed the two Italian-looking men seated by their waitress. Oh, how they loved her. They were drooling all over the place.

"How disgusting," Gerdy winced, "sure if I had those set of 'twins' I'd get all the attention." She was envious of the bosoms their waitress sported. "They're probably fake, look how they point straight out, betcha she could float with those things." She quickly forgot about that, mesmerized by the one man who reminded her of an Italian lover from one of Melva's books.

She could tell they had some money to afford those obvious posh suits, she just knew they were wearing some type of Armani, or something of that quality. "This place must be authentic if it attracts those *kinds*." She mumbled to herself, referring to Italians actually going out for Italian food. She didn't think the other guy was that good-looking, nor was he ugly; he was something in between — defiantly not her type though. He was huge; at least carrying around an extra hundred pounds, but he had a gentle face, like a teddy bear almost. He knew how to dress, subtract the pounds and get rid of some acne and he'd be good to go.

"Hey, look over there Paulie, someone snakin' ya," Gino noticed Gerdy checking him out as soon as he and Paulie walked in.

"Bullshit. Sit down and let's order," Paulie growled and sat down.
Gino sat down and was about to pull his jacket off when Paulie noticed he forgot to leave his gun in the car.

"Why do ya have your piece in the restaurant? Planning on shooting someone?"

Gino felt his gun, "Nah, just forgot I had it on, ya know I sleep with her, too." He laughed while patting his side.

"Betcha got a name for her too, huh? Man, you need to get laid … no worries we'll find ya somebody soon — let's order." Paulie snapped his fingers at the waitress while Gino dove right into the complementary breadsticks.

"Paulie, tell me about the plan you been boastin' about to me … it's off the record ain't it?"

"Yeah, off the record." Paulie scooted inward more making sure no one was listening in (Gerdy and another couple were the only ones who could have heard nything), but he made sure all was between Gino and himself. "Remember when we went into the library and there was the top floor where those stairs led to?"

Gino nodded his large head, "Yeah, what of it?"

"There my *Compagno*, my friend, is where I'm going to have my business." He stroked his hair back triumphantly. At the library, he figured no one would suspect anything going on other than a bookstore and to Paulie this was a superb idea.

"It's not a 'hot place,' right?" Gino was worried it could be watched by police.

"No, *goombah*, it's a freakin' library, use your *testa*! Think my friend, think!" He 'smacked' Gino on the forehead.

Gino continued to pry the rough plan out of Paulie, Gino had to know since he was Stallinoz' *consigliere*, but Paulie was a little unsure on what exactly he'd do there, once he owned the place. He knew that he would have to get some information from someone as to where to proceed with renting or buying that area out. Most likely, the city would have to rent/sell to him; he needed to speak to that ditzy girl who worked there and see if she knew how to go about this.

"The plan, my *Compagno*, is still in the raw, but I do know for sure that I'll have to sell some books to pull this off," he waited for Gino to object to any of this.

Books? Gino arched his eyebrow, a little surprised; this was totally out of the norm for them both.

Gino stopped in mid-slurp of his pasta, "Sell books, eh? That is something different." He peered at Paulie for a moment. "*Cosa Nostra*, this thing of ours ... would be legal?" he asked suspiciously.

"No. Well, the books are legal," Paulie smiled and sipped his vino.

"I'll sit down and talk to Mr. Stallinoz, or I'll call him, this way you don't get your hands in a mess trying to pull this off without approval, okay Paulie?" Gino squirmed in his chair, because he knew this guy was determined to do his own thing, regardless of circumstances within the *famiglia*. "Remember Paulie, you're in a tough spot and you don't want to go against the don in any kind of way. If he approves then so be it, agreed?"

He didn't need anyone to approve this for him, but he knew he'd have to give the don something to gnaw on so he'd stay out of trouble. He wanted to prove to them that he could use his head and make great decisions on his own. He looked around, sipped his wine and stayed quiet; reassuring himself all he needed was to start this ball rolling. And once that happened, he'd be on his way to bigger and better things.

After Melva threw a hissy-fit at Gerdy for ordering her dinner and wine, and complaining that the veggies in the primavera would give her gas all night long, she talked a little bit about the mysterious man in her life.

"So, what's his name?" Gerdy asked while finishing her last drop of merlot.

"I don't know, it's not like he wore a nametag or something," Melva responded facetiously.

"Bitch," huffed Gerdy.

"What?" Melva shocked by the name-calling.

"You're a smart-ass. You know that, Melva?" She was ready to leave; she had to get up early tomorrow to open for Earl. "Next time you see this gorgeous man ask him for his phone number. Nowadays it's not so presumptuous, right?"

"Well, he did let me fall on him, right?" Melva giggled.

"Just be yourself," 'god help us'— she mumbled to herself — "and you'll be great."

"Okay, I will. Oh, you should see him Gerdy, he would remind you of one of those guys you see on the cover of a romance novel, well, except he's got short dark hair opposed to the long locks they have, and he has big dark eyes. And I did see his cute butt through his expensive trousers ..." she grinned wickedly. "And he smelled so wonderful; I could have eaten him all up then and there ... even while Dragon Lady Lomechick watched disapprovingly." She snorted at the personal joke.

"All right, got it all then, let's go — I'm beat. Earl will have my ass if I'm the slightest bit late in the morning."

They summoned the waitress, and then Gerdy paid the bill. As they were leaving, Melva became obsessed with a piece of lint on her sweater. She was looking down at her chest while they walked and she passed by Paulie and Gino without noticing the two men. Gino kicked Paulie under the table, "Hey Paulie there's that crazy broad, ya gonna talk to her *now*?" With one fast movement, Gerdy and Melva were out the door and into the Mercedes.

By the time, Paulie realized who it was it was too late; he was standing on the idewalk staring at the speeding car heading toward the downtown lights, *"Malendizione! 'Damn!* Missed her again, but not tomorrow, *babbo."*

Gino patted his friend on the back, "No sweat *Compagno,* we'll get her tomorrow, :orner her if you have to, but get her to talk … you know be nice, too." He smiled exposing a gold canine tooth. They jumped into Gino's '57 Chevy and sped off.

"Feel like doin' some shooting?" Paulie asked.

"Sure, but my nonna don't want us comin' in too damn late, she'll throw my big fat ass out for sure, yours too, *Compagno."*

"Man, you really need your own place; maybe I'll buy you a place soon, with all the money my plan will make." He was hopeful and sure of himself. They sped off into the countryside to find a good place to shoot.

After they made it back to Nonna's house, Paulie was tired and frustrated at the fact that Melva slipped through his Italian fingers again. Damn he was irritated *and* horny.

Gino thought best to sneak out again and give some more tips to Stallinoz, about Paulie's plan. For Paulie to go do his own thing without full authorization was just dangerous, anyone to do this would surely be 'broken,' demoted in rank. Gino didn't want this to happen to Paulie. Paulie had a great future in the *famiglia* as long as he didn't screw it up. After all, they were only in Catswillow to visit and watch over Nonna and wait for the organizations to meet, and then discuss plans the two *famiglias'* had for business.
His cell phone vibrated.

"Salve, Godfather … I have news, not to say bad, but not good." Gino giggled nervously and cautiously.

"Gino, *consigliere,* tell me, what's Paulie done," Carparillini wanted to hear it from Gino that the rumors were true, before *he* sent out a 'contract' on the young soldier, since he had named himself "Boss." His plan would be in place soon; no one needed to know this yet, least of all Gino.

"He is young and probably in love, he sounds like he's using his dick instead of his head … he only wants to get this broad in bed." Gino inhaled nervously and just then realized he wasn't speaking to his boss, but his underboss.

"I already know about the broad. She will not be our problem for long." Carparillini assured the nervous Gino.

"I need to speak to Stallinoz himself, I thought I was talking to him … him directly is who I discuss this with, not with you."

"*Consigliere*, you are in deep shit if you skip ranks, besides all that is said will be repeated to the don – no need to worry – your words will be clear. Just take care of things until I get a hold of you next time, then we'll see how things will go. Now, tell me the plan."

Gino's instincts had him skim through little details. To Carparillini, sounded like Gino had it all under control and that Paulie's plans were merely a joke, really. Gino never really trusted the underboss totally, something always gnawed at his insides with this guy. But, he had no idea of Carparillini's devilish plans.

"Just keep an eye on Paulie as you're told to do, *consigliere*, and you too will be better off just listening at this time. I will be in touch again soon. Things needed looking into with the Castocci *famiglia*; you are not keeping any information from our *famiglia*, are you? If you hear anything, I advise you to call me."

Gino wanted to oppose all instructions put upon him by this underboss, but thought better to play along for now. He wanted to know where the don was, and why the underboss was presumably walking in his shoes with lay outs of plans such as these.

He knew there was a big meeting with the Castocci *famiglia* coming up, but didn't know exactly what day this would go down. With talks within ranks, this *famiglia* taking over made him a little nervous for Paulie *and* him. Not to mention keeping his nonna out of harm's way – this was always priority ever since he had taken his *Omerta* with Stallinoz.

There was talk that the Castocci *brogata* had a new boss, but no one dared ask; things such as these would come out in the open at organization meetings – usually, they did – but, who knew this time, all the shit tossed around and Stallinoz was not available.

Gino was tired of all the crap he wanted some answers.

Gino mustered up some balls, "Yeah, I'll think about gettin' back to ya." He clicked off the phone down quickly, as if Carparllini would jump through the receiver and kick his ass.

He was tired and hungry, again.

Chapter Six

Melva already had the day from hell at the library, and it was only 10:00 am! When she arrived back at her condo last night, the answering machine was blinking frantically. It was Lomechick telling her to be at the library very early, because she had business to attend to at the Community Center. Her feelings of kismet rushed back just as they did the day before, but she dismissed it all by running a hot bath and contemplating whether or not she should call dear ol' Aunt Bertha for a substantial amount of money. This way she wouldn't have to endure anymore of Lomechick's commands. Let Auntie take care of her — well, why the hell not?

People were everywhere. And rambunctious kids ran up and down the stairs like complete lunatics. And where were the 'parents?' "Oh yeah," she reminded herself, 'they' were all there letting their monsters wreak havoc on the 'new girl' behind the desk." She's constantly pissed off. She was up to her eyeballs in provocation on this Friday. "Aren't Friday's supposed to be a good-mood sort of day?" she sighed.

She was nauseated again. She thought maybe she should go see some kind of specialist: a gastroenterologist (for her colon issues), or neurologist (since she was tingly all the time now), or as Gerdy would suggest, a psychotherapist. *Gerdy should be the one going*, she concluded. She felt so much out-of-sorts it wasn't even funny. She worried she was experiencing an out-of-body experience right at this moment. Melva felt the walls caving in on her and rush up to that favorite room in the building. The restroom.

Gino and Paulie drove up to the library to "clock" Melva.

"Do you really think she's brainy enough — this crazy-ass broad of yours — to really be involved in other things besides this here library, Paulie?" Gino drove around cautiously through the parking lot, hoping no one took interest in them — like the cops.

"*Compagno*, you just never know, so we watch her 'till I'm comfortable with the surroundings, *capisce*?" They decided to park and watch for a while. Paulie noticed Melva's shiny Mercedes parked at the end of the lot all by itself.

"Gino, that's hers," he pointed out the car.

"Nice ride," Gino stroked his dashboard, "nothing like mine here, but it'll do. His finger followed the curves of the dashboard.

"Paulie, you gonna go inside today? If ya go man you need to get something done, like try and get in her pants or something." Gino devilishly laughed.

"Yeah, well, you're not the only one thinkin' that *Compagno*, I have to be slow 'bout this. I want her to trust me; you get the trust thing with these women, or not? Remember that flame you had with the dancer broad, she trusted you until you shot her ex for saying hi to her out on the street."

Gino scratched his large head, "Oh yeah, boy you remember a lot *goombah*." He chuckled. "Yeah, I banged her few times, but she wasn't good enough for my nonna. And after the shooting, well, she wasn't so hot after my body like before." He placed his hands on his chest and remembered that the sweet old woman had wrapped him some sausages for lunch today. Nonna somehow forgave him for his despicable behavior the night before. "She met her one time ya know… it didn't go so well with Nonna. Nonna saw right through her, and gotta have that approval, ya know?"

Paulie shook his head and smiled, "You're stupid."

Gino slapped him on the back and they both had a great laugh down memory lane.

"What you say we go in, take the broad to the back of the library and talk to her, wouldn't hurt nothin', right?" Gino asked feeling his crouch. He was getting a hard on thinking about the freaky broad.

"Yeah, let's see what she's all about … one thing I don't like is that 'problem' we have with that Brinks dude; we may have to 'whack' him if he gets in the way, got it?"

"Uh, Paulie we doin' no whacks unless it's Johnny Big Bones, he'll be the one doin' the 'whack' if there's one to do, *capisce*?"

Paulie was mad. He fought to get to the point where nobody was doing his work for him. If there was a problem to solve, when it concerned his plan, he would do the hit himself. He sighed angrily and looked at his good friend. "Gino, you trust me, right?"

Gino nodded his head, his dark eyes fixed on his *Compagno*. "Just do what you need to do with this girl and get the plan rolling, and I'll step in and spot your back, okay?"

Paulie tapped his friend's head, "now that's what I call a good plan … let's go in and see this girl and her extra space upstairs."

Paulie and Gino stood at the door amazed on how the library mimicked a damn circus, Melva the Ringmaster nowhere in sight.

"Do you see your broad, Paulie?" Gino just wanted to go upstairs and scope out the area, and sit for a while to enjoy the sights of women coming and going.

"I don't see her anywhere. Where in the hell could she have gone her car's out there." Paulie walked to the desk and noticed the empty office behind it. "No one in there," he felt a tug on his pant leg.

"Do you know where my mommy is?" The snot-nosed kid squeaked fretfully.

"Hell no kid! Beat it, before I have Gino eat ya!" Paulie laughed and clearly had a good time scarring the kid. Didn't take much to make kids scream, (his sister, the one he never saw, had one back in Italy, spoiled beyond belief that kid), who was scared of him. Paulie scoped the library some more while Gino hovered in the corner trying to hit on a woman way too young for him. Hey, anywhere the opportunity arises was the best time for both of them.

Melva came rushing down the old stairs unaware of who was waiting for her at the desk. Gino spotted her first and whistled a low sound to Paulie to turn around. Melva had on a tight pencil skirt and matching sweater in her favorite color, pink. She sported some black pumps Aunt Bertha sent her from Milan when she was there last year, and many bangle bracelets that sounded just like a cow's bell when she walked.

"I shouldn't have worn these bracelets they don't go — what kind of idiot wears five different bracelets?" She scolded herself while walking down the stairs in a hurry afraid someone would report her to Lomechick for going to the restroom *again*. She thought she'd tidy up the books in the adult fiction section and then dust; she was excited. She didn't notice Paulie until it was too late …*Oh crap there's my husband!* She squealed inside her head.

"Hey, how's it goin'?" Paulie looked right into her eyes and waited for her to melt. He knew his own sexual powers.

Melva felt her heart palpitations increase. She was going to die. She didn't know if to run and hide behind the large shelves, or talk. Just as she was about the say "hi," Lomechick rushed in like a herd of elephants. Lomechick had decided to come in after all, she was nervous leaving Melva alone for too long.

"May we help you, sir?" Lomechick offered her help to Paulie; she didn't notice Melva standing beside him. "Oh, I see you're already being helped." She spotted Melva, who decided to stand directly in front of Paulie. She smiled and thought he was a dashing young man, but dangerous.

"No, ma'am, he just needs the back room. I think he left something there yesterday, so I'll go and check and show him to the room, thanks."

Lomechick strutted off to her office and slammed the door. Paulie turned to Gino who was busy feeling up his new female friend.

"Hey!" Paulie motioned to Gino who had wondered off with a young blonde woman.

"I'll call you some time all right, gotta go now," Gino bid farewell to his female-candy and walked to meet Paulie by the desk. "How's it goin'?" Gino asked Melva who was still stunned that her fantasy was here in front of her.

She cleared her throat, "the room … you … needed … it's right over there." She quickly turned and headed toward the non-fiction section of the library. *Stupid cornball. Stupid dork.* She was mad at herself for stumbling with her words.

Paulie and Gino just shook their heads in disbelief on how someone they were "clocking" could be so strange, but she didn't know she was being clocked and a soon-to-be *goumada,* mistress.

"Eh, Paulie, did you ask for a room, what the hell is she talkin' about?" Gino shrugged his shoulders, he was totally confused, and picked at his teeth.

"All right, enough of this shit, it's now or never. I'll be right back, Gino. Go wait for me back there man."

Gino reluctantly agreed, "Okay *babbo*, but if she ain't talkin' then grab her and take her out the back door.

Paulie just glared at Gino, "Get outta here, or go back there, man. I'll be back." He followed Melva who was still talking to herself. He signed heavily and wished he had a cigarette.

When he found her, she was on a stool straightening the shelves. But, he could see the shelves were fine. He shoved his hands in his pocket and placed a broad friendly smile across his face, "You doin' all right? Can't help but notice you look like you're ready to leave this joint."

Melva wanted to disappear and at the same time lusted for him. "Oh … I'm okay, just trying to keep the place nice for our nice patrons such as you." She laughed nervously and cleared her throat. "Do you need any help with anything, or can I show you something?" She realized how that sounded when the handsome stranger arched his eyebrow. "I mean, do you need me for anything?" Again, she was fumbling what to say — he made her crazy! She was stunned when he answered.

"Yeah, wanted to talk to you, is there a place we can talk? — That back room you were talkin' about would be okay." Her eyes, big as the moon, reflected her amazement that he would want anything to do with her ... much less talk to her. She didn't know what to do, so she did what Melva did best ... panic. As she was about to run, Paulie grabbed her arm. She didn't know what to do; she thought she already loved him, but to touch her...

Paulie noticed the horror in her eyes, "Sorry." He let go of her arm. "Just like to get to know you is all, so how 'bout it?"

Melva looked up at him, "You want to talk to me? Why?"

"Hey, lady, I'm no maniac, okay? I'm just a guy wanting to talk to a girl, you." Paulie was exhausted already and hadn't even done what he came here to do with her. He bet that that friend of hers felt the same way with this girl. She sure was some piece of work.

Melva contemplated for a moment: shelve the books evenly, dust the filthy shelves, or go with the tall handsome man. Gerdy would have her ass if she missed this opportunity, so she decided to go with him. "What could happen?" she wondered. She panicked again.

"Wait, I'm supposed to be working I can't just walk out. Mrs. Lomechick will fire me for sure ... see my first day was yesterday and ..."

Paulie couldn't believe this broad, and all the work it was taking to take her outside to talk.

"Wait a minute ... what's your name?"

He asked again. "What's your name? — Mine's Paulie. He extended his masculine tanned hand.

She felt her stomach flip when he took a step next to her. His voice was like velvet, chocolate velvet. And he smelled so good! Her heart was beating and surely, he noticed her sweaty palms and forehead. *My makeup!* She was horrified that she might look like a sweaty pig.

" … My name is Melva … uh … nice to meet you Mr...?" She took his hand and kept it for a minute.

"Just call me Paulie."

"Great. Paulie." She repeated his name as if in a spelling bee.

"Great place you got here," Paulie sniffed around and looked Melva up and down.

"Glad you like it; see it's really old and has a great history behind it …" He never took his eyes off her, looking her over like a grade A choice of beef. *Can he see through my sweater?*

"No history lessons for me, gorgeous, just want some help on something, if you don't mind," intuitively he watched her for he knew what her answer would be.

"Well, sure. What can I help you with, I'm all ears." She giggled and motioned her hand to her ear. *Idiot.*

All Paulie knew is that this would most certainly be a challenging, "talk."

Now that she knew that he wasn't about to rape her in the non-fiction isle, or anything like that, she felt a little more comfortable with him all the sudden and agreed to meet him when she closed the library this evening.

Lomechick made the excuse that one of her farm animals was sick and had to rush home to take care of it, so Melva agreed to lock up again. She was so excited, she didn't even keep in mind that she wouldn't get to the dusting she needed to do by the following week. She couldn't deny the communal animal magnetism they shared; this scared her, because she really hadn't been this attracted to someone this forcefully … well, only once if you count Gerdy's egotistical and geek-of-a-cousin, she slept with one time, which was one time too many.

Chapter Seven

Melva glanced at the large clock hanging on the wall across from her, it was a quarter after eight and he still hadn't shown up. She felt an awful feeling in her stomach, but quickly disregarded it as just nerves.

Gerdy had given her pointers for her date earlier when Melva called asking her to go check on Brinks when she got to the condo. She just knew he'd be "starved" by six o'clock. Gerdy agreed eagerly, because she too wanted just to go home and call it a day.

Most of Gerdy's customers today had been the worst she'd ever seen: hollering obscenities at one another, griping about their latte's being too hot/cold — no one was satisfied whatsoever, she attributed it to the full moon. She had a split-second thought about stroking Brinks upon her arrival there, because she'd heard by petting these ungrateful creatures they would bring relief after a horrible day. Brinks might bite her, but she'd take her chances. "Here kitty, kitty." She called the king of the condo. "Damn cat, where are you?"

Brinks sat perched on the sofa arm, in kitty-gargoyle form.

It's my house. What in hell do you want? And where's my food!

Gerdy noticed how Mr. Wide-Butt hung over the side of the couch and shook her head, "You really ought to think about kitty-aerobics or something."

Melva paced the library floor practicing her Brinks catwalk, just in case she needed to walk toward him for any reason. *Now how does he do it? Oh yeah, he crosses one paw at a time in the back ... no wait; he crosses the front ones too. Oh God, I'm so confused!* She noticed a spot on the wall and walked over to it, and moistened her finger, and began to smudge the ugly mark off the wall. There were a few books sticking out of the shelf, uneven, so she thumped those back into place. Then she noticed Lomechick's repulsive stacked desk and thought of a brilliant plan. She was excited! Melva began stacking papers by dates; then she stacked papers by category: committee, city plans, grants and book lists.

"Oh how wonderful this will be when it's done. Lomechick will be so surprised; I might even get a raise." She beamed. As she pulled out a drawer and a piece of used straw flung out, she fell back. "Oh how gross!"

She dared not to touch it, not even with her shoe. Swiftly she reached for a tissue that was in a box at the bottom of one of Lomechick's bookshelves and picked it up very carefully, as if it were a breakable valuable item. "There's something on it, I'm going to be sick." She quickly ran to the exit.

There to meet her was Paulie dressed in a casual tailored ensemble. He looked like he had just stepped out of Armani's website catalog. He smelled crisp and clean, as if God had lovingly showered him in a forest of evergreens.

Oh, god does he look and smell great! I think I'm in love! Help me stay calm. Oh, and look sexy too ... don't forget that! She pleaded with her Maker.

He quickly looked around, and then pushed her against the circulation desk; not taking his eyes off her, he waited until he had her where he wanted her and then spoke.

"Where's the john at?" He was so close to her, but he wanted to wait that part out – the seducing part.

Melva only moved her head, "it's up the stairs," she pointed toward the mysterious upper floor.

He smiled, "I'll be right back, or do you wanna help?" He waited. He was serious and winked at her.

Am I about to have sex with this hunk right now? Birth control? But, I don't have any. Shit! Double shit!

"Uh, I can show you the way if you want me to, or hold the door closed for you." *Why not unzip his pants for him, Jezebel!*

He knew he had scared her a bit. "No, *goumada*, after I 'go' you can show me the stuff upstairs, or is that off limits?"

He stepped forward and could see how amber her eyes were, like a wild flame he'd never seen before.

What did he just call me?

"Yes, you can see whatever you'd like, *mi casa, tu casa.*" She tried her best Spanish and giggled like a school-girl.

"Oh, hey, I don't speak Spanish, sorry." He turned his head and giggled to himself softly. *What an airhead ... pretty airhead.*

She started up the stairs, but froze. She was nervous about him scoping her out from behind, but she remembered all he could see were curves, nothing else. After all, they weren't even dating. As she walked up the stairs, she could feel her ass on fire; the stares were coming in full throttle! She turned around to make sure her new "friend" was okay.

Damn right he was okay, more than okay. He smiled wickedly at her. She caught him with a fixated eye gaze on her curvy-derrière.

"There's the restroom. I'll wait right here for you, okay?" She went and stood next to a column post, arms at her side like a soldier guarding the Queen of England.

"I'll be right back, is there a light up here, or we gonna do this in the dark? — I can't see a damn thing."

Do what? Oh god!

"Sure, I'll find it," she hurried around kicking at boxes and nearly toppled over some books to find the switch.

He went into the restroom and she began to scan through the room that she only saw while running to the restroom.

There were treasures beyond belief in the musty upper room. Old poetry books and boxes upon boxes of old literature stood dangerously stacked in the middle of the room. For someone who collected old novels this was heaven! She noticed a box marked **Various Authors**. "Um, bet there's some great stuff in here." She bent over slightly to look inside the dusty box and made mental note to get some damp paper towels for her hands. There were oodles of old hard-backs, including one of her favorites: Mary Wollstonecraft Shelley's **Frankenstein**.

"Oh my god! This is mine now!" She screamed and jumped up and down.

"What the hell did you find?" Paulie stood in front of her and realized he never seen anyone this excited before about a damn old book. He wanted to reach out to the ditz, but he refrained. Timing was everything.

"Oh, Paulie, look!" Melva handed him the dusty, smelly book. Who knows how long it had been in the stack of old boxes.

"You like this stuff?" He scoped it out and recalled watching the movie when he was younger.

"Well, don't you? It's like the best, well, Dracula's the best, but this is pretty darn close." She thought she'd better calm down, he might think she was crazy.

Too late.

"Are you gonna keep it?"

"Ooh, what do you think? I mean it's not exactly mine, yet. Maybe Lomechick will let me have it after I donate some money. I think she'll let me." She decided to sit on top of some sturdy boxes, but remembered the towels she needed first. "I'll be right back okay." She sped away.

He walked around and sniffed the air; it reminded him of an antique store he would visit back home when he was younger. You just knew the 'old smell' as soon as you walked in. His grandmother's house smelled of that and espresso. He missed his *famiglia* back in Italy, maybe he'd go back in the near future, and maybe take this broad with him. He grinned.

"Okay I'm back," Melva adjusted her skirt and saw Paulie staring, again.

"Sit. I got an idea." He wasn't one to beat around the bush.
Before they sat down, Melva cleaned an area for herself, and cleaned another for Paulie.

"I gotta know you wanna help me, or what, *goumada*?" Paulie made sure his voice was smooth as silk when he asked. He also made it a point to touch her knee with his.

His dreamy, delicious dark eyes mesmerized Melva. She held **Frankenstein** close to her chest, her breathing raspy; she didn't care what he wanted from her, but she hoped it was naughty. Her amber eyes trailed his face and down to his jaw, then to his neck where she could see his pulse (she wished she were a she-vampire so she could suck-suck him dry!)

"Hey what's wrong with you?" Paulie snapped his finger in her face.
She wanted to kiss him, but she wondered if it was too wonton to do so, especially on their first meeting-date. *If it were a full-blown date — then heck yeah!*

She shook her head, "Oh, I'm okay … uh, just a little hungry is all." She lied.

"Sorry, *goumada*, didn't even think of food," he touched her soft face with his hand, "so, what's it gonna be, you gonna help me, or what?"

"Oh, yeah, sure thing Mr.…uh, Paulie." She smiled sweetly.

Oh, shit, what is it I'm going to do for him?

Chapter Eight

"Listen, if you want sex, well, I can't say it'll happen —"

"Yo, lady, hold on a minute — slow down, we'll get to that, but not right now."

We will?

"Oh, sorry, my bad," Melva snorted.

How romantic.

Paulie couldn't believe this was happening so fast. Yeah, he burned inside for this girl, but he wasn't so sure he wanted to get involved romantically just yet. He knew this one would want romance, especially after he saw how excited she got about the damn book. He fantasized he could drape himself in book paper and let her do naughty things to him, but he had to make sure this Brinks guy wasn't gonna interfere. He'd have to take care of him first.

Paulie got up and paced the upper floor. "I need you to help me find out who owns this building. Is it this Lomechick woman?"

"Oh, I don't think so, but wait … she might, her family owns half the town."

"So, who'd know?" He looked around and picked up an old novel by Herman Melville. "Moby Dick, huh? This is about that whale and shit, huh?" He couldn't remember if in Italy he read that while in school. He doubted it; he was too busy hanging out with Uncle Frankie, a *capo* for the Stallinoz *famiglia*. He played a *cugine*, as long as he was around his favorite uncle and learned all he could. Now he would do things for himself, the boss — well; he'd deal with that matter later.

"You read the book, huh?" Melva asked, ecstatic that her soon to be man was a reader.

"Nah, I don't think so. So, you are going home, or what?" Paulie was tired of all the books; it wasn't what he had in mind. What he really wanted to "do" was Melva against the wall or on top of the boxes.

Melva looked around uncomfortably and tried to keep the conversation up.

"Do you want to meet again and talk about the building?"

"Yeah, sure. Tell ya what, talk to that broad you work with about the building 'cause I need to get this rollin' soon, okay?"

What rolling?

I wonder what Brinks is doing? Poor baby of mine, I hope they like each other ... what if Brinks hates him.

Spaced out she finally answered him. "Okay, I'll ask her, but what if she doesn't tell me anything? I've only known her couple of days now and I'm not exactly sure that she cares for me, you know?" She nervously licked her full pink lips, which got him even harder.

"I'll handle her if she gives you any shit, *abbastanza bene*?"

"Uh, okay?" She didn't know what that last part was, but took a guess at its meaning. She made a mental note to check out a book tomorrow on Italian phrases. She wanted up-to-speed language help with her newfound lover.

Paulie cleared his throat and shrugged his broad shoulders. "I'll walk you to your car, c'mon." He was about to reach for her small hand when she darted up the stairs. *Pazzesco donna, crazy woman!*

"Dove va? Where are you going?" He shook his head while he watched her run up the stairs in her tight pencil-skirt.

"I'll be right back, just have to wash my hands — dirty," she giggled and continued to run up the stairs. Melva's heart was racing when she entered the restroom.

She wanted so much to ask him over, but she knew that was not the right thing to do, she wanted to take it slower. And when she got home, she would have Brinks smell her cheek where Paulie had touched, so that he could get his kitty-smell in, and get used to his scent.

"I look horrible! No wonder he wouldn't kiss me." She sniffed her underarms. "Gross." She did the best she could to tidy up and cursed herself for forgetting her purse downstairs. "This will have to do." She looked into the mirror and did a primp pose and did her best 'Joey from Friends' expression, "How you doin'?" She felt ridiculous.

"Hey, you come down soon?" Paulie yelled up at her, impatiently.

She swung open the door and walked toward the stairs. She swished her hair around a bit, "sorry I took so long ..."

Totally ignoring her efforts Paulie opened the large doors of the library.

She hurried and grabbed her purse and keys to lock up. She felt Paulie up against her ... very close he was, indeed. *Oh my god, he feels so good.*

Paulie noticed her tense up, again. "Don't worry; I'm not gonna rape ya. I just want to feel ya before I go, that's all." He was direct.

Melva could feel his hot breath against her ear.

Paulie slid one hand up her thigh, then pulled her tightly close, "You like?"

"Oh … uh, yeah …" She dropped her purse on the ground and had to bend over to get it.

"Don't do that, *goumada*, it's not fair. I've still got my clothes on." Paulie smirked and he then let her go.

Melva fumbled with her purse and keys, but managed to get the doors locked. *I need a cold shower.*

Paulie did too.

He walked her to her Mercedes and patted her on the butt. "Take care, *goumada*. I'll see you tomorrow, don't forget me." With that, Paulie was gone.

She figured he must live some place nearby. She slowly got into her car and dialed Gerdy.

Gerdy was relaxing next to a sexy plump young male. Brinks. Brinks purred and loved the way Gerdy stroked his fur this way and that. Some felines would oppose this awesome rub, but not Brinks. This feline was in heaven with his tuna-smelling babysitter.

Gerdy glanced around Melva's condo and noticed the entire movie collection was cult classic movies with Bela Lugosi, Lon Chaney or Christopher Lee. "What a damn drag, Melva." She was irritated with the selection Melva had to watch. She should have brought over her own collection of blood and guts, the way movies were filmed nowadays gory and stupid, in her opinion. As she was about to disturb the "sexy guy" from his comfortable spot to grab a movie, Melva's home phone rang.

"It's your mother," she sighed as she reluctantly answered the phone.

"Melva's whore house, how can I help you?"

"Gerdy! What the hell? — don't answer like that; it could have been Aunt Bertha, you know she'd have a cow," Melva huffed, but then gathered herself and thought about the great news she had to share with Gerdy about Paulie.

"So … you do not want a whore tonight?" Gerdy giggled and winked at Brinks. *Aunt Gerdy is so cool. I should know I'm a cat. And I know cool.*

"Listen Gerdy I'm on my way home. How's my boy doing? Did you even remember to feed the poor thing? Did you mess up the kitchen?" She noticed while driving out of the parking lot Paulie was nowhere in sight.

"Nah, didn't mess nothing up, oh yeah, just the bedroom. I had my way with Brinks. He's quite the ladies' man," she laughed and opened the cupboard to see what else she could eat.

"Gerdy, I think he really likes me."

"Who, Brinks?"

"No, Paulie." Her insides started to tingle. She turned on her heated seats to warm up "down there."

"Oh, gawd, tell me you did something besides talk tonight. I didn't watch this wad of fur all night for nothing. Did ya?" She opened a box of pop tarts and started in on them, skipping the toaster.

"Are you eating?" She winced at the thought of the sure-to-be mess Gerdy was making a mess in her kitchen.

"Neeww, wheeff?" She mumbled, spreading crumbs all over the place.

"Liar. And don't feed Brinks any he hates them. I'll see you soon." With that, she hung up and floored it home to clean up.

When she entered her condo all the lights were off except the old Victorian lamp, Aunt Bertha had sent her a while back, thinking it went with all the other Victorian furniture she'd sent her. It was important to Aunt Bertha that she have a comfortable place to reside when visiting her favorite (only) niece.

Aunt Bertha thought she was English. She had the accent down, although it came and went just like Madonna's. Melva humored her and went along with the English accented- conversations. Aunt Bertha's last husband, Leopold, was the English gentleman, so Bertha figured she would be the proper English wife from Florida. Born and raised there, but she thought she could adopt a much more sophisticated tongue. She went to live with Leopold and began her transformation, and she fooled everyone except Gerdy. Gerdy knew Aunt Bertha when she lived in Florida, when the whole family would visit out there on various holidays and towed Gerdy along to keep Melva company.

Gerdy and Brinks were snuggled up with Bela Lugosi on the tube claiming his prey.

"Aw, this is so cute!" Melva went to the plush couch and held out her arms for Brinks to jump in. He did not.

"Hey, guess we dozed off," Gerdy said. She still had crumbs on her chin from the pop tarts, and Brinks had leftover tuna on his whiskers.

"You both ate in here?" Melva began to dust off the couch and coffee table with her hand.

"Here, I'll clean my own mess. Tell me about the date, I have ten minutes I can spare. I need to get to bed, remember I got a job to go to in the wee hours."

"Gerdy, it was so spectacular, our chemistry, I mean," she sat down and hugged Brinks, who then bit her on her finger and dashed out of the room, and headed toward his own room.

"He's so sweet," she ignored her cat's sour attitude, "okay, sit back and relax while I tell you everything."

Chapter Nine

Gerdy plopped down on the oversized Queen Victoria chair, reached over and grabbed a handful candy from the martini-styled dish. She spat.

"What the hell is this?" She screamed and nearly choked.

"Oh, that … it's Brinks snackums, just a little something when he's a good boy. Now, he doesn't get them all the time, mind you." Melva tucked her legs to her side, and made herself comfortable on her couch.

"Melva are you freakin' crazy? You just tried to poison me with this crap!" She ran to the sink and held her head under the faucet, and gulped down water by the mouth full.

"Come on and sit down, I'm trying to talk to you. Anyway, you should have seen what he was wearing. Girl, he looked good. I couldn't concentrate at all, but we did get a chance to talk about books and stuff. Oh, wipe the sink after you're done in there, you know, water stains."

"I knew it! You bored his fine ass off. Way to go goofy," Gerdy picked her teeth for any last bits of cat treats still stuck in there. "So, when are you sleeping with him? Because I'm bored hearing about your inconsequential bedroom escapades that may never even happen."

"Gerdy, I just met the guy. What am I a slut? — She held up her hand, "don't answer that. Just because I slept with that cousin of yours, doesn't make me 'easy.' Besides, I think he just wants me to help him with something important," she started picking stray hairs off her sweater.

"Like what?" Bored, Gerdy started to think of what she had in her frig to eat. Bored again, "Melva, I told you that he was in the mob or something correlated to that, don't make me say 'I told you so,' okay? Just watch yourself; those kinds of guys aren't easy to get rid of, *if* you happen to change your mind."

"How do you know? Are you a pro at dating mobsters? Gerdy, I really don't think he's into anything illegal. Actually, he just wants to buy the building that I work in, that's all."

"You airhead, do you know honestly think he wants that old building? Boy, you'd have to be blind not to see what he's after. Call it woman's intuition; you do have that, right?" Gerdy shot her an arrogant glance.

Melva didn't like where this conversation was headed. She was not an airhead. She wasn't blind to the man, even though his powerful muscle and his gorgeous locks of hair coated her thoughts with lust, but she felt pretty confident that he wasn't into mobster stuff. And even if he was, these days it's not like Al Capone. She was sure she didn't need to be afraid of him, or his mysterious, stocky friend. She really liked him and she wouldn't let Gerdy scare her into not liking him, she'd have to give him the benefit-of-the-doubt.

"Gerdy, I don't like you stereo-typing him at all, you barely know him," she crossed her arms and stared across the room, really wishing her friend would be more supportive.

"Oh, okay, I'm not sorry though. Just be careful and call me, I can always borrow a small handgun from Earl." Gerdy looked at her and knew she scared her out of her Jimmy Choo's.

Melva shot up and grabbed Gerdy's arm, "You're out of here, now go!" She shot her a smile and knew Gerdy was pulling her leg about the gun. She hoped.

"Night then, lock up behind me," Gerdy said feeling the protective vibe.

"Goodnight, and thanks Auntie Pussycat for babysitting," Melva snorted loudly out in the hallway. She closed the door and headed down the spiral staircases that lead to her library/office. She felt the urge to send correspondence to her favorite Auntie Bertha.

When Paulie arrived at Nonna's, the smell of calamari still lingered, but he knew damn well all of it was gone. Gino the pig ate it all up in two seconds flat, no doubt. He walked into the parlor area of the old house and sure enough, there was the pig laid out comfortably on Nonna's recliner. He went over and kicked it hard, "Hey gotta talk, wake up."

Gino's eyes blinked, "Wha ... the matter? Nonna?"

"No. Wake up *goombah*."

"Hey, yo Paulie, when did you come in?" Gino staggered off the chair, and straightened his wrinkled slacks as if he were going somewhere.

"Sit down," Paulie kicked his leather shoes off and sat down on the couch.

"What's wrong, man? Date go all right with the ditz?" Gino sat down again and noticed Paulie's stern look.

He lit up a cigarette. "Went okay, I guess … she's hard to figure out, but she's nervous as hell around me, don't like that much."

"Damn, Paulie, did you try stuff on her, or what. Huh?" Gino sent Paulie a devilish grin.

"Nah, nothin' like that, *Compagno*. Want to play it low for now."

Gino looked confused. Paulie could have his way with any female from here to Italy if he wanted. Was this ditzy broad taking a hold on him that would make Paulie think twice about using someone? He hated to think this woman "broke" Paulie's streak. To him, Melva was not much to write home about, but then again, some women just have "it" in them and can take an extraordinary man like Paulie and make him into a big gob of jelly.

"Wanna talk about the plan you got for the books?" He offered.

"Nah, just one thing … tomorrow we'll head out to the library again, and if we have to we'll talk to this Lomechick woman there, she's the head tuna there, that's what *my goumada* says." Paulie stretched out and put his hands in the back of his head, and got very comfortable. He thought about Melva's soft skin and of course, how her ass looked in that tight skirt. He doubted he could hold out for much longer without taking her right there in the library. Maybe he'd find him a nice room in the back, secluded, where he and his *goumada* could get things nicely done.

"You hear how you talkin', *Compagno*? Talkin' as if she's yours, you don't know her, and you want her involved like this? I'm nervous Paulie, with all these damn females involved. You remember Big Bones is comin' next week; we got lots to get squared away before our 'beef' goes down about the situation with Castocci *borgata*."

Since neither Gino nor Paulie knew of Stallinoz leaving New York abruptly, they just figured the meetings were still taking place when Big Bones came summoning them back to New York. They had no idea that things were about to change for all involved.

Gino still felt in control over Paulie despite Paulie's strong actions to take things into his own hands, but he knew that his good friend would not make mistakes. He'd watch Paulie throughout the years from *cugine* to now, and knew Paulie had special qualities to make a damn good boss some day, if it were in the cards for him.

"Don't mess with me right now, Gino I know what I'm doin' and nothing's going to happen with the females, I can handle them, remember I'm Paulie-the-freakin'-great!"

He got up and headed toward the kitchen. He washed down some milk and headed for bed. Nonna was hiding behind a door listening to the whole conversation, and when he walked by to get to his bedroom, she whacked him with her hand towel. "What the hell —"

"Santo Cielo!" Nonna attempted to swat Paulie again. Just as she was about to strike Gino took hold of his little nonna.

"Nonna, please! Paulie didn't mean nothin' about any females being hurt," Gino pleaded with his feisty grandmother.

Nonna apparently didn't take to the idea of her fellow-women citizens being involved in any of the perilous events about to take place around Catswillow.

Gino took his nonna back to her peaceful sanctuary at the back of the old house and then came back up front. "She heard it all, man and she ain't happy with me, and you … well, she doesn't like you very much anymore. Paulie, she's gonna write to you mamma."

"What the hell for? I swear I need my own place and quick," Paulie hoped the old bat wouldn't write home to Italy, because the short, cute Italian woman there would surely cut his balls off. His mamma wouldn't mess around. "Shit and I was going home after all this got squared away down here, now what? Tell her not to write her, *Compagno*, please. My hands *and* balls are tied, damn-it! I'm going to bed."

Gino thought it was pathetic that he and his friend were afraid of these women. But, he knew the impressive power of Italian women. Gino followed and went to bed himself.

Chapter Ten

Castillo Stallinoz, placed in the Chianti region, within beautiful Tuscany, tempted most to steal a glance, or better yet try to sneak a peek inside its massive walls. The muscular guards that surrounded the *Castillo* intimidated tourists. Tuscany's infamous Mafia 'Boss' was in residence this time of year.

Mr. Stallinoz had abandoned his New York sky rise apartment for the time being. He had much to deal with, including the Castocci *brogata*, who were trying a complete take-over of the entire organization. The word was they had a certain high-ranking member helping them out. Stallinoz had a feeling it was Carparillini.

He wasn't happy with things in the small town where he'd sent his *consigliere*, Gino, and he wanted to make certain he was in a place where he could concentrate on things and at the same time, he'd enjoy his true home.

As the Boss was in a foul disposition, his administration felt the need to meet at the Tuscan *Castillo*.

The Boss stroked his Persian feline with his jeweled hand.

"We have problems that need attention gentlemen, why haven't those problems been resolved?" He looked around the lion-clawed wooden table for answers.

"With all respect, Boss, I'd like to know where *Consigliere* is and why hasn't the matter been looked into before now," Carparillini, his underboss, demanded. He was irritated lately no one shared those decisions.

Stallinoz sat up straight and placed his feline companion on the Tuscan rug.

"You my friend, need to find Frankie, *capisce*?" He glared at his underboss.

Carparillini cleared his throat and spoke firmly. "He is to be sent to Catswillow within the day. I've made certain he will be on the plane. I will send his crew with him. Does this please you, Boss?" he asked this with a newfound air of arrogance.

Stallinoz stood up and then placed his cigar in his mouth, headed toward the large window that looked out over his vineyard. "You speak to me as if you know exactly what needs to be done. Why not do it yourself?" He continued without expecting an answer. "Does Frankie have power? No, he does not – what he has is one nephew that goes against the *brogata*, therefore must be dealt with swiftly. And, the girl, who 'clocks' her?"

"Scusi Boss, she's been taken care of … no trouble with her. Gino said she's Paulie's *goumada* now, or soon to be. She's no threat …" Carparillini stopped mid-sentence.

With one swift move, Stallinoz was standing with his cigar on one member's hand. The man yelped in pain as the others watched; no one dared object to this action. The Godfather could do as he wished; they were all guests in his *Castillo*.

"You find me Frankie, Paulie and the girl, and I want them brought here – Gino, I will deal with later. My *consigliere* has much to answer for. When you find Frankie, give him the 'contract' out on his nephew, no one goes about plans themselves, he will learn the hard way. "*Mi lasci in pace!* Leave me alone! Now, go." He sat down and swiveled his leather chair around to face the window, with his feline companion once again on his lap.

One member looked over his charred, painful hand he was marked to do the job his boss instructed him to do: Find Frankie. This member knew exactly where Frankie was.

Each member, including *capos* and their soldiers kissed Stallinoz' jeweled hand as they left each proclaiming, "Godfather."

Stallinoz felt a presence within the room. The room was large enough for one to go unnoticed behind a massive piece of furniture, perhaps. But, his well-keyed instincts let him to know when someone was there. "Carparllini, is that you?" he asked without turning to face the doorway.

"Yes, my friend, it is I." Carparllini sat down next to Stallinoz, no one else was in the room, or so it seemed.

"What is it you need now, Carparllini?" He didn't look at his underboss, just stared out the window.

"My friend, it is time for a change in the organization," he paused a minute pondering how to put his next step into words. He thought about actions … *they do present a more swift response than words would.*

"Forgive me Godfather, but your time has ended."

Faster than Stallinoz could eat a bowl of pasta, his life was taken with a steal blade. The two men that held him down were hiding behind tapestries; near the favorite window of the one, they called 'Godfather.'

Stallinoz' favorite Persian feline managed to escape the whole murder. Her sixth sense, kept her nine-lives intact for a while longer …

Chapter Eleven

"Hey, Big Bones you leaving today?" Frankie, *capo*, asked as he cracked his knuckles at the blindfolded man sitting in the middle of the floor, blood drooling out of his mouth. This man was a Rat, and Rats are whacked swiftly.

Big Bones had arrived in New York a few days after receiving the burn mark on his hand and instructions to take care of things in Catswillow. "Yeah, *capo*, better get it done soon. Got any words for your nephew?" Big Bones stood there in the musty old basement by the bloodied, dead man and kicked him with his pointed boots.

"Tell him not to screw this one up, or I won't be there to help him anymore — oh, don't let on that I know about the chick. When I get there, I'll take care of that problem. Go." He gave instructions in Italian to the two men hovering in the corner, and then grabbed a pack of cigarettes from his sleeve and began to smoke. The room was quiet now, just as he liked it, which gave him space to think about his next move. He knew all he needed to know about his nephew's escapades in order to make the decision to move in, and take care of things himself. Paulie was his favorite nephew, but the *brugad* was most important.

Chapter Twelve

Melva sat in her home library looking around the bookshelves trying to see if anything was out of place, she knew Gerdy had been in there, evidence by cracker crumbs that were around where she kept some of her favorite old movies. She also found a Dove bar wrapper in the trashcan beside the half-moon shaped desk. The decorated trashcan was just for looks, not for trash. She thought that fact was obvious. In the back of her mind Paulie popped in, naked, sprawled out on her bed. The blankets covered some of his muscular parts, but mostly revealing his strong thighs …

"Meow!" Brinks came in as if a bat-out-of-hell with his tail puffed out like a feather duster, eyes large and round.

Melva stroked her pussycat, "Want Mamma to love on ya for a bit?" Brinks hissed and jumped down and knocked over a cat figurine that was on top of the desk. "Boy, are you in a pissy mood! Gerdy must have really done something to you to piss you off." She walked around her quiet little library and tried to pick out a racy romance novel she hadn't read in a long time. She had a plethora of vampire/werewolf novels she adored reading, especially Sherrilyn Kenyon's paperbacks. She finally picked one out, turned off the lights and headed up to her bedroom.

In her luxurious bed with her furry-male at her ankles, morning was indeed her favorite time of the day; here with Brinks, she couldn't think of a happier place to be … Well, just one other place …

She sat up and grabbed her kitty, as he struggled to tear loose from the grips of Medusa, (her hair was wild in the mornings), he flung himself off the canopy bed and onto the carpet. "You're hungry aren't ya? Well, Mommy has to get ready and quick." She remembered Lomechick wouldn't open the library today, something about a farm animal, or something stupid like that.

She padded to the bathroom to take a shower where the overly snippy feline met her there. Brinks nipped her ankle a few times and meowed angrily. "Okay, cat, I'm coming, I'm coming!"

Brinks circled around like a buzzard, ran between her legs, which made it even tougher to get to the kitchen in a hurry. She poured Brink's favorite crunchies in his bowl that read The King. As she headed back to the bathroom the phone rang …

"Hellooo!" Her aunt Bertha sang sounding like Mrs. Doubtfire.

Melva winced. "Hello there, Auntie, where are you at my dear Auntie?" She quickly adopted the pristine tone that amused her aunt.

"I'm on my way on holiday, dear child, come to see you. This, I gather, is all right with you dear." She didn't wait for the answer. "Good, good. I shall have my driver dash me to the airport — Melva dawling, you should see my plane, it's fab — it's absolutely fabulous!" Bertha sensed something … "Child, did your 'friend' come this month? Is this why you're grouchy?"

"Oh, no, Auntie, I'm fine, really I am. Just running late for work, not good you know. But, tell me when are you expected to arrive?" She needed some coffee and soon!

"Yes, yes, I'll be there most likely in a day or two; must pop in on my girlfriend from London — oh, oh, do be a deary and grab me some biscuits and tea from that local bakery so that I have something for my mornings out on the patio. Thank you, you are such a doll, ta-ta dear. I'll call you again when I'm zipping through traffic." Bertha giggled excitedly and then hung up.

Brinks sat on the counter; after he made a pig of himself with the "crunchies," (this cat knows gluttony), and licked his paws and face. Melva thought and then noticed that Brinks was reading her mind.

"Oh what are you looking at?" She slumped down on the Victorian couch. ME-OW! He complained again.

She sat there for a few minutes dread encapsulated her body; with Aunt Bertha's arrival, she really didn't have that much time to spend with Paulie. She had made big plans in her mind. Like when would be the right time to ask him over. She could cook for him, well, ordering out was more like it, but now that her aunt was coming – and who knows for how long – she wouldn't be able to carry out her plan. "Damn."

She peeled herself off the couch and slowly walked into the kitchen. She really wanted to stay home with Brinks today; just forget about the conversation and take a long hot bath and piddle around, like Brinks does.

Gerdy always said, "Cats are good for three things: eating, crapping and sleeping. For our amusement, they let us pet them, and don't forget the part about playing janitor with the litter box, oh yeah and food service … the list could go on …."

But, Melva knew the most important thing was companionship.

When she got into her bedroom, she noticed what time it was. She had exactly forty-five minutes until she had to high tail it outta there. She picked out a long, straight chocolate-colored skirt and a golden cashmere sweater that made her boobs stand out, figuring Paulie was coming to the library and would like what he saw. She grabbed a pair of pointed-toed kitten heels to wear with that outfit and jumped in the shower.

Before heading to work, she popped in the small gourmet shop on the square, not far from the library, to purchase Bertha's request for her visit.

A contentious old man on the steps of the old library met Melva. Her stomach tightened; she hated confrontations.

"Good morning. How are you?" She tried to be polite.

Mr. Contentious didn't say anything, just kept looking down at his watch.

Melva finally got the door opened, completely ignoring the old grouch. *How can someone that old be in that much hurry?* She glanced quickly toward Lomechick's windowed office and noticed how filthy it looked. *"Does she ever clean?"* She winced at the sight of candy wrappers all over the dragon's desk and thought she'd better keep that door closed today. She heard a loud bang.

"Hey lady, I'm in a hurry, just check me out."

Not so much is a "hello" or a "how are you? Or, even a kick in the ass. Fine, you're in a hurry buddy, too bad!

"Will this be all? — We have other subjects on this matter, if you want to check some more out," ... she was trying to be helpful and cheery.

"Did you not hear what I said," the old fart grumbled. "This is all I want. You really should listen, instead of standing there like a long skinny pole." The old man placed his hands on his old, bony hips and waited while he played around with his dentures in his mouth.

Gross.

Her day wasn't starting out very well. She looked forward to calling Gerdy and hopefully Lomechick's farm animal wasn't too ill, so she'd show up by noon. She wasn't sure, when Paulie would show up, but figured it was when he got good and ready.

With the grouch gone, it was finally quiet and Melva decided to scan the library, and tidy up a bit. She noticed the children's section in a complete turmoil, like usual. Mrs. Lomechick seemed to be oblivious to the messes around the library.

"She's oblivious to everything it's a wonder she even hears the phone ring. I wonder if she'd hear a bomb if one exploded." Melva was depressing herself. She needed a pick-me-up from Gerdy, right now! She went to her desk and grabbed her cell phone.

"Java Jar," Gerdy yawned.

"Why are you yawning? It's like only ten o'clock. Hello?" She didn't hear Gerdy breathing.

"What the hell do you want so early?" Gerdy's head hurt.

"Ouch! That was rude, what's wrong?"

"Oh, nothing, I've just been here for four friggin' hours already."

"Sorry. Guess staying up late didn't help either, huh?"

"You don't say … what's up, Melva? Are you getting ready for a break already? You may want to wait until Earl gets back." Gerdy chuckled. She was her ol' self again.

"I do not think so. That man's a pig, honestly, he's so rude and I don't think he's like that to everyone, right? — Don't lie, Gerdy! He hates me, and for what?" She didn't like Earl singling her out like that; it made it hard to hang out at the Java Jar with Gerdy.

Earl came waltzing in humming, wearing a t-shirt that read 'LIFE IS TOO SHORT To Cook For You People.'

"Gerdy, you taking an order, or are you talkin' to that whack job?" Earl spoke into the receiver so that Melva could hear him loud and clear. Earl and Gerdy giggled.

"I'm not a whack job! That was so uncalled for I'm never ever stepping foot into that nasty coffee place of yours. Do you hear me?"

"Okay, calm down. He's just messing around, Melva. Where's your sense of humor? Boy, you do need to get laid …"

"Who's getting laid, that old prune?" Earl yelled back from across the coffee shop.

"What? What did he say, you better tell me, Gerdy." Melva fumed.

"Nothing, he's just kidding around, really." Gerdy walked around the counter to sit down. "When's lover boy coming?"

"Not sure," Melva answered.

"Are you all right?" She knew she let Earl get to her. It didn't take much to do that.

"Yeah, I'll be okay gotta run, bye." She really didn't get the pick-me-up she needed. With Aunt Bertha on the way and no way in hell Paulie could come over and have his way with her, she felt melancholy, again.

A few hours passed with the occasional piqued patron: bitching about fines, nothing on the shelf to check out, or just simply in a bad mood. She'd had enough, and to top it all off Lomechick came charging in like a deranged animal; it was plain to see her farm animal was in peril although she didn't elaborate on the situation when asked.

Melva was in the back section of the nonfiction section shelving and having a good time straightening books when she heard the voice of an Italian god. Paulie.

Paulie walked in looking like Gary Grant, but Lomechick was the one that greeted him, not Melva.

She watched in horror as Paulie kissed Lomechick's callused hand!

She nearly fell face first as she sped from the back to the front desk, dodging patrons to get up there quickly.

Out of breath, "Hi Paulie," she puffed. She steadied herself with one hand on the counter while she primped her hair with the other.

"Hello. If it's all right I'd like to talk to your nice chief Librarian in private." *Oh ... My ...Gawd! He cannot be serious!* But he was.

Before she could say anything, they were in the windowed office chatting away like old friends. She hated it; *her* god was not for sharing. She had completely forgotten that Paulie needed Lomechick's information on the building, captivated by Paulie powers that made her a blubbering idiot, which didn't help matters.

After what seemed to be an eternity, Paulie came out of Lomechick's office with a triumphed smile on his gorgeous face.

"So, all went well I presume?" Her voice was a quivered with hurt.

"Oh yeah, got the man's number right here. You know she was a big help, you're pretty lucky to work for her, no?" Paulie was sincere, but badly mistaken.

"You are not serious, are you? She's the one that hates me, since day one, which was just this past week." She didn't want to talk about Lomechick; the old goat looked like she'd been in an orgy and loved it.

"What's wrong, *goumada*?" Paulie sensed his girl was perturbed.

She inspected a book obviously damaged by the previous borrower. "Oh, nothing, just that I wanted time to visit with you too before you left."

"Where am I going?" Paulie was confused.

"Can you stay a bit and chat?" Her amber eyes sparkled.
He leaned back to see if Lomechick was busy in her office.

"Yeah, I can stay … there's that back room, is anyone in there?" He pointed to the storage room tucked in the corner of the downstairs area. Books, VHSs, and DVDs were stored in there for easy access.

She dropped the old dog-chewed book.

They walked over to the room and she peeked in, it was a musty room, but room enough to 'chat.' She was giddy.

He grabbed her ass with both hands and began to kiss her neck. All at the same time kicking the small door closed. He hiked up her tight skirt and felt his way up toward her thigh searching for the wetness her body was sure to have by now.

She couldn't believe how good he was with his hands and how quickly she was aroused. Guess she must have felt the tingles when he walked in the library!
She didn't know what to do with her hands so she ran them through his dark thick hair.

He moaned, and mumbled something in Italian, which made her even hotter.
He feels so good …

His hand found her bra and unsnapped the front closure. Her breasts sprung out like two happy young sisters going to a carnival. He licked one while covering the other with his hand. He sucked and sucked. Melva couldn't wait any longer.

"Paulie, take me now!" She spread her legs farther apart. She remembered the dirty desk she was on, but then decided, "Who the hell cares!"

"*Goumada*, I will." Paulie gruffly answered.
Then a knock vibrated on the door …

Chapter Thirteen

Lomechick peeked into the tiny storage room, "I thought I heard voices. Melva are you in here?" Lomechick could see Paulie adjusting his belt and slicking his hair back and messing with his collar. All she saw of Melva was the top of her head from behind the desk, which stood in the middle of the room.

"Yes, yes Mrs. Lomechick I was just … uh … showing Paulie our collection of DVDs and so forth. He wanted to donate a few things."

"—Okay, okay, enough explaining, just get back to the desk. Patrons are waiting to be checked out and they are impatient today. With that, she turned on her heel and was gone.

She smiled up at Paulie's crouch, and then stood up with his help.

"I was for sure she'd catch us. Oh my god, I cannot believe we were this close," she gestured with her fingers.

Paulie ignored her overreactions to the whole thing and just simply kissed her hand.

"It's okay, don't you worry, *goumada*. Now, I gotta run and you gotta go do whatever it is you do around here. He kissed her passionately and walked out before her, looking around to see if there was anyone else lurking about.

"So Mr. Palazollo you want to rent out the top part of my old building? Is that correct?" A plump man with a brown polyester suit asked Paulie, who sat directly opposite him, in a stuffy, cigar-smelling office.

"Yeah, that's right. And I can get ya six months' rent tonight — if we got a deal." The plump shyster peered over his glasses and then reached for a fresh stogie. He offered Paulie one, too. He refused.

"Well, being that you know my old cranky-assed sister-in-law, the librarian, I think I'll take your offer." He grinned exposing a large gap that you could run a locomotive through.

"Can I ask you what you plan on doing up there?" The shyster leaned back in his office chair.

"If I tell ya, I gotta kill ya," Paulie chuckled, but was serious.

"Ah, a stern business man, I respect that. Good luck to you, but don't screw me with this rent, got it?" He pointed his stogie at Paulie.

Paulie got up and walked to the glass door, "No, *you* don't screw with me, that's how it really is. *Arriverderci, figlio di puttana!*

"What? What does that mean?" The shyster sat there dumbfounded; maybe he should have asked Lomechick more questions about this guy.

It was late by the time Paulie reached Nonna's old house; he had a beer at a local bar, and then decided he was hungry. He could smell Nonna's home cooking and scent of cigarettes in the air. He saw a car in the driveway, which didn't belong to any one of them, and then he remembered Big Bones was due in at any time.

"Hey, Paulie!" Big Bones stood up; he was a lot taller and stockier than Gino, which put Paulie at a good three-inch disadvantage.

"What's going on, Bones? Where's Uncle Frankie? He is comin' in soon?" He pulled up an old chair from Nonna's retro avocado-green kitchen table and turned it around, and sat down, arms leaning over the back of the chair.

"Nope, no Frankie this time. He sent a message, but you know me and my mind — forget things from time to time," he grinned at Paulie.

"Don't believe ya, so where the hell is he?" Paulie's temper was rising, and it didn't help he still had a hard on for Melva from earlier today.

"Don't get cocky with me Paulie, you have no idea the shit you're in for goin' and doin' stupid shit on your own." Big Bones glared at him.

Paulie glanced at Gino, who was just sitting there like Jaba the Hut picking his teeth. He felt something was up, but didn't think Gino would rat him out.

"Oh yeah, so what do ya know," Paulie waited.

Big Bones ignored Paulie, "I hear we got ourselves a problem here in Pussywillow …"

"That's Catswillow, dumb-ass." Paulie was in no mood.

"Oh yeah, well I call is as I see it and it's got a lotta pussy here," Big Bones laughed and nodded toward Gino, who was still picking his teeth.

"When are you leaving?" Paulie wanted this fat bastard gone. The lack of news about when he'd see his uncle made him even madder and was all he could think about, well, except his new bookstore *and* Melva of course.

"Mr. Stallinoz, wants to know what deal you made, so I suggest you get back to him and have that sit-down and get things out in the open, eh?" Big Bones grew tired of the conversation and he had other matters to attend. He left in a matter of minutes, but not before Gino's nonna stumbled into her kitchen from her night out playing bingo with her friends. She flew at Gino with her purse and cursed him.

Paulie was beat mentally and physically, sexually frustrated, too.

The week has passed eventfully for Melva. Gerdy and she made up after the whole fiasco with Earl. She just didn't go into the Java Jar, unless he was out of town.

Paulie started cleaning up his rented space and it was amazing what he did in a matter of weeks, and he had help, too. Eager, pleasing women helped men that looked like they stepped out of the GQ magazines. Paulie trusted the men, who were part of the organization. Paulie knew all of them for many years. Some of these men would stay here in Catswillow to operate the bookstore, since Paulie seriously toyed with the idea of going back to Italy to see his Mamma.

The women that came into use the library lingered longer than usual Melva noticed; they just wanted glimpses of the gorgeous hunk running up and down the stairs.

Paulie had a designer come in and redesign the layout of the top floor, like put a door where the stairs met the top attic. Melva would have to go through that door in order to go to her favorite place, the restroom. She didn't mind, she'd have that chance to steal a kiss from him, if no one was looking, and if dragon-lady Lomechick was not there.

Books came in from all over, but Paulie did take Melva's advice and stocked some old literature throughout the store. As soon as he showed a profit from the bookstore, he'd use the *clean* money to channel through to place a gambling joint in every other basement in Sicily, just like he and Frankie talked about doing for so long.

On the last evening of perpetual cleaning and storing up in the loft area, he was completely beat. He hadn't seen much of Gino, but then no one had. He figured Gino went out and found him some slut to hang with and pass time since he had been so busy with Melva and his enterprise.

He noticed Melva by the circulation desk; she was bending over to grab something off the floor, most likely lint. He reached over and grabbed her waist.

"Come over here with me …" He led her to the small dark area just under the stairwell.

"What … are … you … doing?" She was already breathing heavily with his strong hands caressing her. She had on a looser skirt, which made his hands more free to roam.

"Don't move. Let me do something …" he pulled one of Melva's legs and placed it over his hip, and slowly sought out his wet-prize that lay between her legs. He noticed she had on a garter belt, so she wasn't wearing the difficult pantyhose she wore last time. He loved these …

He started to feel his way up her crisp white collared shirt and began to unbutton a few buttons to reveal Melva's golden-tanned breast, he had no reservations about placing his mouth on her chest just then. He tasted her with his tongue and glided over her nipple, he wanted to put the whole thing in his mouth, and then the other.

Melva felt his Italian-rod against her, and she wanted him inside her at that very moment … but then realized they were still in the library!

"Paulie … stop, just for a minute, okay?" She tried to pull herself together.

"What's wrong? I thought you wanted this, was I wrong?" He arched a perfect tanned eyebrow.

"Oh, boy, uh, I have to check on Brinks —" Before he could stop her, she was heading toward the circulation desk where she kept her cell phone.

"Brinks? What the hell for?" He pulled himself together.

"It's okay, really, I'll get Gerdy to check on him and we can —"

"Don't bother *goumada*. I'll catch ya later." He walked out of the library without a second glance.

"Damn!" She stomped her new Prada heels on the carpeted floor. A few patrons were gawking at her and Paulie.

"What? Never seen a Librarian … mad?" She called Gerdy, who was at home enjoying some bon-bons she purchased at the store earlier. She figured no one was paying attention to her figure, so why should she.

Melva sniffed, "I really blew it, Gerdy. He walked out of here like I'd done something wrong."

"What the hell did you do now? — 'cause I know damn well you did something to that Italian lover to piss him off. Did you try to clean him with the vacuum cleaner?" Gerdy laughed, "Or wait, wait, you asked him to wash his hands before he touched your ass, or something else — no doubt — ridiculous like that."

"Are you quite done? No, nothing like that, he's pretty clean, actually. That's one of the things I love about him … he smells wonderful …"

"Okay, well, I gotta run, my bon-bons are melting, and this conversation so not worth that."

"Would you do me a favor and check on Brinks, I can't remember if I fed him enough to last him through supper. Please?" She begged. Gerdy had a key to her condo, so she knew that wouldn't be an excuse.

"Fine, I'll feed the furry prick … uh, prince, I mean." Gerdy clicked off her phone. She was relieved; her boy would get supper and a nice visit from Auntie Gerdy.

Lomechick had made herself scarce just after eight o'clock, so it was up to Melva to get the library in order for the next day.

She finished tiding the library and still felt terrible about what happened earlier with Paulie. He really had her juices flowing. And what would he do to her with that tongue? She wanted to find out. She just hoped she hadn't blown it. "It's as if mentioning Brinks set him off," she wondered why. Maybe once he met him he'd appreciate Brinks, too.

She was struggling with her purse when she heard a horn honk and turned to see who it was, hoping it was Paulie. It was Aunt Bertha. Arriving a day too soon at that.

Good grief woman, why today!

Bertha flew out of her black and silver stretch limo. Just as she was set to arrive on the library's steps to give her niece a hug, two thugs came out of nowhere and grabbed them both. The limo driver was hit over the head and dumped out onto the parking lot floor.

Chapter Fourteen

Paulie was already near Nonna's house when the thugs attacked Melva and Bertha, so he had no idea of their perilous situation. All he knew was that he felt sexually frustrated and tired of hearing about Brinks; he would 'whack' him tonight. He thought about it and decided to call Melva first, maybe she'd put something sexy on for him that would be nice. Better yet, he decided just to pop over unexpectedly, have his way with her, but first 'whack' Brinks—and throw his ass out! He knew where her condo was since him and Gino 'clocked' her a few times when they first met. He'd head over there after he grabbed a beer.

Melva's head hurt and she couldn't feel her legs. What she did feel was something very heavy against her back. She tried to move, but it was too painful. She tried to speak, but only her inner monologue was present. She blinked and tried to make out where she was. Where was Aunt Bertha? She turned her sore neck and saw her aunt's head bent down. *Oh god, she's dead! Just great, after I cleaned the place up and had her special teas ready for her, she goes and dies on me.*

Bertha moaned a bit.

"Auntie, are you all right?" She moved her shoulders and then her fingers trying to see if she could get free from the ropes that were digging into her flesh.

"Oh ... dear ... I think I am a tad bit ... thirsty," she turned her head to see part of Melva's face. "Oh, good it's you. Be a dear and try to reach for my flask; it's in my coat pocket."

"You want a drink *now?*"

Bertha nodded her head 'yes.'

"For pete's sake! Oh, all right." She wiggled a bit and managed to turn her whole body toward the left. She reached as far as the rope would let her, and felt the binding gripping her hand that she was using to dig around Bertha's pocket. "I've got it!" Just then, the flask slipped out of her hand and hit the cement hard, revealing the owner's name on the front: Leopold Froggenhall III.

"My Leopold's flask, Melva, look what you've done!" Bertha started whaling.

"Auntie, best be quiet now, because I'm not so sure our captors want you drunk. It's better this way. Honestly, do you really think liquor is the answer?" She rolled her eyes. Only the walls witnessed her irritation.

Bertha was livid. Her drink was gone, she was strapped like a horse to a stall, and she needed to pee. She tried to go to a "happy place" without her flask contents (it was just a little vodka, no harm in that really), but to no avail …

"I'm wondering child, why is it that we are tied up? Have you any idea?" Bertha regained her proper-bred woman composure.

She wondered now why men would do this to her and her aunt. She never thought about Paulie once. She just hoped Gerdy would have sense enough to go and feed her cat.

Bertha snored. Melva nudged her.

"Sorry dear, long flight. I sure could use a spot of tea right about now," Bertha wiggled a bit in her chair that she was constrained to.

"Sorry Auntie, no tea time today," she was hurting and started getting a little scared. Just as she started to talk with her aunt three men walked in, armed with rifles and one of them stood out considerably.

One man looked very familiar to her amber eyes. *Why, could it be … Paulie?* It was not Paulie.

"*Non me ne importa un cavolo,* I don't give a damn! Just untie the broads, now!" Frankie cursed and wasn't happy having to leave his territory, and come to the small town to clean up his nephew's messes. In his opinion, Big Bones failed to carry out his one task. Frankie thought, "If you want something done right, do it yourself."

She studied the handsome stranger a bit. He looked like Paulie and had some of his mannerisms, but her man didn't have a permanent scowl across his face.

"Melva dear, do not, and I repeat do not give out any information about us. You know, like where you live and that you have a wealthy auntie … oops."

"Auntie, do you really think I'm *that* stupid as to let them know everything about me? Just sit tight, no pun intended, and let me do all the talking." They had no idea that Frankie was standing next to her chair.

Bertha felt her niece tense up. "Oh dear, he's behind me isn't he? Please sir, she's an old spinster, she has no husband and no children, well, if you count that silly wad of fur she calls a cat, but don't kill her!"

"Hey! —Who said anything about killing? Oh god, don't kill me! I'm too young — Hey, who you calling spinster. I recall dear ol' Auntie you married quite old —"

"*Basta*! Enough already, you're giving me a damn headache!" Frankie felt the side of his temple with one hand; the other hand rubbed his neck. "Women."

He knelt down to talk to Melva face to face, "So, you're the *goumada*, eh? Guess you'll do," he smirked as if he'd defiantly seen better. He traced his finger down and around her whole face, "Guess he could love you, but what about if I ruin this pretty face of yours, what then?"

I don't know if I want to answer that.   Paralyzed with fear, she didn't answer.

"What do you know *goumada*? Tell me." He waited. His dark eyes danced around her face.

You, Mr. Smarty-pants are not nice. Hope you don't invite yourself over for Thanksgiving supper either.

"My nephew made the mistake of getting you involved with the *famiglia* businesses, you know that?" He kissed her cheek.

It felt like a rat kissed her and she squirmed in her chair. "I know absolutely nothing about your nephew, only that he's a gentleman, not an ass like you!" She was irritated and meant every word.

"Oh dear, Bertha winced sinking deeper into her chair.
He reached for his handgun.

"Have it your way, *goumada*. You will talk, or you'll never see your aunt alive again, got it?" With that, Frankie left the cold basement.

One tear left her exhausted body. *Paulie where are you?*

Paulie had his beer and grabbed a piece of focacia bread that Nonna had baked and headed down the road in Gino's car towards Melva's condo.

Gerdy looked at the time and noticed it was way past 'his royal highnesses' supper; he'd be ticked off for sure, "he's a cat, of course he's pissed," she fumed to

erself slipping on her moccasins she had purchased at a flea market some time ago. And
ossed on a worn out bathrobe for good measure, and headed out the door.

Paulie parked along side of the road to create the element of surprise for his
oumada, not that she knew what Gino drove, but he thought it was clever enough. He
ecalled the garage with the number eight and headed up the public access stairs.
Walking down the hall, he recognized the frizzy-haired woman in front of him …

Gerdy sensed someone behind her, but thought nothing of it; if he was a rapist
ne'd better watch out, she was PMSing and it was not a pretty sight! She turned on her
neel when she got to Melva's door.

"Hold it right there, buddy boy, I've got a gun," she tapped her smelly robe
pocket. As soon as she said that, she recognized him! —It was lover boy! *Holy hell what
was he doing here?!* She smiled exposing some chocolate she had forgotten to lick off
her front teeth.

"Hey, is Melva home? I wanted to see her for a minute."

"Dude, she's not here. I'm just here to check to see if Brinks ate is all; she'd have
my ass if I didn't check on him, gotta have his damn tuna or else." She shook her head
with plenty of aggravated attitude as she opened the door to the condo.

His 'Excellency' met them at the door.

"Yeah, I'd like to meet this Brinks, sounds like a real prick if you ask me."

"Well, there he is," she pointed towards the fur-ball, "all in true furry-form,
wonderful sight isn't he," she reached down to pet the fur-ball who hissed at his auntie.

Paulie was dumbfounded, "A freakin' cat?" He pointed at the cat, with the
attitude 'I'm better than you because I'm a feline.' "This is Brinks? A frickin' cat?" He
put his hand over his mouth and laughed.

"What's so funny?" Gerdy wanted in on the joke.

"I was gonna 'whack' this little guy, ain't that a bitch?" He laughed again whole-
heartedly.

They both had a good laugh, at Brinks' expense of course.

Laugh some more I have claws people! Brinks was not humored one bit.
But then again when do humans humor cats?

Chapter Fifteen

The phone rang when Gerdy was placing tuna down on the counter for Brinks; supper had been late, so there was hell to pay.

"Hello, Melva's house of whores," she snorted and mouthed to Paulie, "she hates when I do that."

"Put Paulie on, Gerdy," the voice at the other end demanded.

"Who the hell is this?" Gerdy fumed, not recognizing the voice at the other end.

"None of your damn business just do it!"

"Fine!" Gerdy stomped toward Paulie where he was sitting.

"It's for you, can you believe that?"

Paulie could believe anything; that's just the way things were for him with this business and all. But, he didn't expect *this* particular person to be at the other end of the line.

"Yeah ..."

"*Salve*, my nephew."

"Hey, Uncle Frankie, how did you get this number?" He suspected Melva's phone and apartment to be tapped also; his mind was working overtime to be one-step ahead of his uncle's, this was one thing Frankie taught him as a young *cugine*. In his gut he had a bad feeling something was up, if his uncle had this number then most likely, he had this address. But, he didn't want to go and jump to any conclusions, yet.

"We need to talk, and I want you to know I'm very upset that I had to come all this way to talk about this *minchioneria,* foolishness that you have gotten into. You know how the business works, and I'm afraid you're in deep shit kid."

"To hell with it all! I can do well on my own, *capisce*. I don't need any of you coming in here to help me out with nothing, you got that Uncle?" His hands were sweating his neck tightening. He was fed up with people telling him what to do like some circus animal.

Gerdy was nervous. She could tell it was a heated telephone conversation. *Boy, are these Italians hotheaded or what. Hey, I wonder how he knew who I was. I told Melva not to get involved with the Mafia! Now I'll have to save her ass from all this crap. I wonder where she is, oh ... my ... gawd! —I bet he's got her some place!* Her heart was racing; she had a terrible feeling he had Melva. She looked down at Brinks, who all the sudden looked like an innocent cherub in an English garden. Poor thing didn't know it, but he may have to live with Auntie Gerdy if they didn't find his mommy.

"I've got something you may not want damaged. Bring me the 'skim' and it'll stay 'off the record,' I guarantee your safety you're *famiglia* after all. I'll expect you soon and don't be stupid, Paulie." Frankie didn't wait for any objections he just hung up.

Paulie placed the phone down, but he didn't feel defeated — far from it in fact. He would undoubtedly have to rescue Melva at all costs. His emotions were rolling in many directions and he didn't like it. When he arrived in this small town, he had no idea he would meet this girl and her upside down life, but he knew he wanted to keep her just where she was, in the center of his heart.

"I've gotta go," he headed toward the door, but first he kneeled down to stroke Brinks, who was still as a statue for at least thirty minutes right by the door.

Brinks hissed and spat at him.

"He likes you, can you tell?" Gerdy laughed nervously.

"Thanks for letting me in, see ya," he pulled the door open.

"Oh no ya don't, I'm comin' with you!" She placed Brinks on top of the Victorian couch, "good kitty, and stay," Gerdy had an agenda.

"Look lady —" Paulie tried to object.

Gerdy bulldozed her way out the door passed him.

"Are you comin'? Close the door, oh here lock it up," she handed him the keys to lock up and all the while he stared at her as if she were crazy.

"*Pazzesco donna*! Crazy woman. Fine. You really got a piece on ya?" Thinking she didn't.

"Piece? — Oh, a gun? Yeah hold up." She ran to her condo, raced in, ditched her robe, retrieved Earl's gun he had lent her and locked her place up. "Okeedokie, ready or not here comes Gerdy, ready for action."

"You're braver than I thought carrying that piece of shit around," he looked at the gun and he laughed, "guess it'll work."

They headed down the street and onto the main street where Frankie said he was keeping her.

"I'm famished indeed!" Bertha fanned herself with the hanky she had stowed away in her other pocket.

Frankie had freed up their hands since they bitched about it for hours now, this was the very reason he never married: Broads and their damn issues.

"Lady, one more word about food and we'll make sure you never eat through that fat lip of yours, *capisce*?" Big Bones barked.

"Well, I never!" Bertha objected.

"Well, maybe that's your damn problem lady —try getting screwed once and a while …"

Frankie tapped Big Bones on his meaty shoulder, "Enough go and do something else. I'm tired of seeing your ugly face.

"Okay, boss." Big Bones looked once back at Bertha and wished he could knock her around few times on her prissy ass.

Frankie turned to Melva who was looking a little pinkish; she hadn't eaten in a while and was starving.

"My nephew has no idea what I have planned for him and you," he laughed devilishly.

Bertha wanted her flask. It had mysteriously vanished from the area where it had fallen earlier. "Can I have my flask back, sir? It's a family heirloom, and I want it back at once."

"Would you like me to call Big Bones back and have him keep you company?"

"I don't believe I want that at this time, but thanks for asking." She replied squirming in her chair.

"You're a smart-ass and I'm getting pretty tired of it," he started to pace back and forth.

If Bertha could do one thing, it was to piss people off, especially men.

Melva reached her hand out to him, "Please, she doesn't know the affect she has on people, if you'd just let her have her vodka she'll shut up, I promise." She felt horrible and thirsty, and wished it were the weekend so she could spend time with Brinks, she missed him and hoped Gerdy was tending to his every whim. Paulie – on the other hand – she really didn't know what to think … she guessed she missed him, she didn't know any more, with his family acting in this terrible manner. Her mind was spinning in all sorts of directions, she just didn't know anymore. She didn't understand it one bit.

She heard Frankie talking to someone perhaps it was Paulie. She really wished she knew. She had always pictured him on his white stallion coming to save her from the evil wraths of Lomechick, but this was a tad bit different. Lomechick would be pissed if she didn't show up for work on time, her first few weeks had been hell and she was tired. She wanted a vacation. She dreamt of white sandy beaches, a Cosmopolitan and sitting with her *Ya-Ya sisterhood-Sex-in-the-city girlfriend Gerdy gabbing about men ...*

Chapter Sixteen

"Do we just kick the door open or what?" Gerdy had an awesome adrenaline rush: Gun in her pocket, cute guy by her side. Well, he wasn't up for grabs, but she thought he still was pretty cool to have around.

"You're getting a kick out of this, aren't ya?" He kind of liked having Gerdy as a sidekick, while he waited for Gino to get off his ass, and took his time about meeting them there. He called Gino on his way over and told him everything that was about to go down. Gino had to beg his nonna for the keys to her Impala so he could meet up with them; this didn't make him happy at all.

"I'll look like a freakin' old lady, *Compagno*," he griped.

"No one's gonna see ya. Just hurry it up, got a chick for a back-up."

"The hot girl with the frizzy hair, am I right?" In Gino's mind, Gerdy was 'doable.' He knew the lowdown about Frankie kidnapping Melva and didn't want Paulie's *goumada* to get hurt; after all, she was an innocent bystander in all this.

"Yeah, so hurry it up!" He clicked the cell phone off.
Gino arrived shortly after they did. He was sweating profusely, and chewing gum.

"What's the matter with you?" He noticed a soaking wet Gino off the bat. His baby blue polyester suit was soaked in sweat.

"Nonna's car is freakin' hot, no damn air condition!"

Gerdy started waving her gun about, "So, when we going in?" The gun made her feel confident.

Gino looked at Gerdy, "You gonna use that thing? Do you even know how?" he asked nervously.

"Yeah, I had lessons —what of it?" She did not lie.

"Hey, shut the hell up you two I hear someone coming," Paulie placed his body firmly against the cold brick wall of the old building, he instructed his counterparts to do the same.

They spotted two men that were dressed in black trench coats; they headed toward a black BMW and took off. That meant only Frankie and Big Bones were left inside.

Paulie knew they could take them both, three against two. Well, maybe Melva had some high heels on that could pierce an eye out or something. If he knew anything about this girl – this would be it.

Big Bones was sitting legs stretched out enjoying a cigar while shuffling some cards in his hand when Frankie walked in.

"You really gonna do something here, Frankie? If you want me to, I'll take care of your nephew for you. Didn't know if you had the stomach to take care of that, ya know being *famiglia* and all but, let me have the young broad – I hate that one." Big Bones chuckled and inhaled his cigar.

"Knowing my nephew, he'll think with his dick instead of his head, so we got no problems. You'll take care of who I tell you to take care of, so don't ask me anymore, just smoke your damn cigar. I got things to think through." He sat down across from Big Bones, took out his pack of smokes, and lit one up. He sat back and relaxed a bit. He thought about how he was the Big Earner for the Family, not Paulie.

Paulie was supposed to follow orders, not give them, and not go against the *Omerta*. He didn't know what he told this woman. He had learned about the broad, she and her friend Gerdy, and something going on at the library. He knew one thing; the bookstore upstairs was raking in some big bucks —this would be his now, that's all there was to it. His men did a good job locating and bugging the area since day one when Gino and Paulie arrived. He just didn't trust either of them, even though Gino was supposed to make sure things didn't get out of hand with Paulie. Gino would have to pay his price too, for not following the rules.

Mr. Stallinoz made that clear to him when words leaked out, and that Paulie would soon betray them all. No-one knew that Stallinoz was no more …

"Melva, darling who do these men want? And why are they so hostile?" Bertha was oblivious a "Mafia thing" was going on in front of her.

"Auntie, don't you see who they are? Dark, tall and handsome – well – except for that blob of a man, that doesn't like us; but that's beside the point. Don't you notice the suits —the language for god's sake?" She was tired of being tied up at the ankles; she wanted to stretch out her feet, hugged in a pair of black and white leopard-printed Manolo Blahnik heels, which were a gift last year, from Bertha of course. She recalled when she got the large box full of designer skirts, dresses and shoes. The card read: For the wild minx in you! She grinned at the memory.

Her aunt interrupted her thoughts, "That friend of yours is just not a good influence on you, Melva dear. It's a great concern to me that you would associate yourself with this Gerdy through all these years. Haven't you got any respectable friends?" Bertha sat with her hands on her lap, flask cradle like a small babe. Something always bothered her about Gerdy ... she couldn't put her finger on it ...

"I do have friends, and Gerdy's not the problem. She pouted, "wait till you meet Paulie, you'll just love him," she said sarcastically knowing Bertha may have a problem with him at first sight; he did look just like their captor.

"Oh, I think I understand; you're friends with this Paulie that this thug wants to talk to."

"Auntie, I'm not so sure they will just 'talk' okay? So, my advice to you is to keep your eyes and ears open, try not to make the big guy mad, or Paulie's uncle. I have this distinct feeling that he'll come and save us. At least I'm hoping he cares enough to do so ... but maybe he just cares about that bookstore and nothing of me. Oh Auntie what am I to do if I was just being used by that hunk of a man?"

Was all of this for nothing – the pursuing – the lust fest they had had in the corners of the library? In every passing minute she grew resentful towards the man, she called her future husband in her thoughts. Since that day he waltzed in, she knew he was the one for her. She didn't care about backgrounds like Gerdy did; she cared about true feelings. He made her feel important. And he didn't hold it against her that she had little quirks here and there – and the odd clinging-love she had for Brinks. Was he a lie that just was passing through her life, and for what reason?

"I sure could use a spot of tea. It's way passed the evening hour, I feel it in my bones, child. That man – if he would only have the decency to get me that cup of tea – I'd forget the whole thing and not summon the police when we are freed from this godforsaken dungeon." Bertha promised.

She patted her aunt's clammy hands, "I know Auntie, I know."

Just at that moment, Paulie burst opened the door. He saw the two bound in their chairs, strapped by the ankles.

He came! He came! I am in love!

Paulie gave them a hand motioned to stay quiet. He glided his way toward Melva to untie her and maneuver her and her aunt out of the building. He didn't want his *goumada* in the middle of any of this; she'd had enough. He guessed her aunt was shittin' bricks by now, poor woman.

He smiled at Bertha and nodded his head at her. All Bertha did was make a 'huff' sound. He accounted her attitude as discontentment for the all suffering that she had just been through because of him. He couldn't blame her for hating him, but perhaps she'd accept him nonetheless – after she would get to know him better.

He knelt down when he got to Melva's chair. She could have sworn he was about to pop "the question," but he didn't; he did untie her though. Finally, she could stretch out like Brinks. Before Paulie let her go, he placed his fingers on one leg and traced her calf, and giggled at the sight of the lethal pair of shoes she was wearing. He loved her *gambas*!

Before he knew it she shot out of her chair and threw herself at him, "I knew you'd come – didn't I tell you Auntie!"

"Hey *goumada*, let me get you and your aunt outta here, fast."
Melva searched his face for answers.

"What's wrong, Paulie?" She wanted so much to be with him, not run away.

"Not now, *goumada*, just listen to me, okay? You and your aunt are gonna leave, but I promise when this night is done you and me – some place hot and romantic – got it?" He winked at her – an irresistible wink – which melted her insides. She nodded; as in a trance that took over her entire body.

He untied his future aunt and looked her over just to see what was in store for him when Melva reached that age.

"Well, I suppose 'thank you's' are in order. Is this what you're expecting?" Bertha asked Paulie, spitefully.

Melva grabbed her aunt's chubby hand, "Not now Auntie 'cause these big bad men are about to fight and we don't want to see all that, right? —Or, would you rather I leave you here with Paulie?" She winked at him. She was clever; he'd give her that.

Chapter Seventeen

Paulie sent Melva and Bertha around the other side door and instructed them what route to take back to her place, and to wait for his phone call. He instructed her to pack a suitcase —and the cat! He didn't want her to be disappointed in him. He was after all her Italian knight-in-shiny-armor a newfound role that he liked. He would keep her safe no matter what the consequences were for him – and there would be – no doubt about it.

She was so beautiful and when all this was over, he'd take her far away from all this, maybe soon he'd get the guts to have her meet his mamma —that was a scary thought. *I hope Mamma likes skinny golden-redheads. I sure do!* He thought.

Gino came from around the corner and summoned Paulie back out the doorway.

"Found 'em, they're in the back room towards the rear entryway, we got 'em, so now whatcha gonna do, Paulie? You know my ass is on the line because of the broad you love so much. What of Nonna and me?" He was as good as dead, they both knew that, but Paulie didn't want that outcome for either one of them.

Paulie knew of Frankie's well-kept secrets and his shady dealings here and in Italy and some throughout Europe. He was a very good businessman. If he wanted all of this to be over – and have something to show for it – he'd have to kill his uncle. He knew contacts that Frankie had at these locations. All he'd have to do is make things legitimate with each one, pay them off a good sum for their silence, and find a nice place to live life out comfortably without any interference. He planned to have a family of his own one-day. This family would be with Melva and her *pazzesco*, crazy aunt.

"*Compagno,* don't worry about Nonna, or yourself. I got us covered. Trust me." With that, he placed his hand on Gino's back to comfort his close friend and nodded his head to continue.

A few minutes later, Gino went back toward the restroom only to find Gerdy standing over Big Bones in the hallway.

"Good job, *compagna*. How did ya do it?"

"I came in here, saw the door open, I stuck my leg out and tripped him, as he fell I thumped him on the head with this here gun Paulie didn't seem to think I could use. See, told ya I knew how to use the damn thing."

They laughed. And a spark between them flickered within each of them. They went to find Paulie, who was now on his way to confront his uncle.

"Hey, good job," he looked down at Big Bones' body, "he'll be out for a while, but he'll be no threat to me after tonight."

"Where are Melva and her aunt?" Gerdy asked, worried about her friend.

"They are heading back to her apartment; I want you both to pack up something fast, we are all leaving when I'm done here, okay —so go!"

Gino went over to pat his friend on the back, "*Goombah*, I'm thanking you right now for what you did for me and Nonna. Wanna know something? I think this broad likes me, too." They both chuckled.

"Man, don't get your hopes too high on her; she looks too tough for ya … get movin'. I'll call ya later. Oh, get your nonna outta town for a while, too. Go."

He strolled into the dark smoky room Frankie was in and nonchalantly sat down.

"So, you had the *coglione's* to come and kill me, eh?" Frankie went over to stand face to face with his nephew.

"Does it come to that, Uncle?" He knew it deep down in his gut it was now, or never. He didn't think of anything but Melva at that moment …

Frankie could feel the hatred running through Paulie. "If you think my associates will tell you everything, then you're a dumb ass."

"You let me worry about that." He popped his neck and shrugged his shoulders, and then popped his jaw.

"I taught you better than this, *ceffo*. You'll never get away with any of this shit you planned out, because you're nothin' but wet behind the ears, Nephew. You know nothin' of this kind of business. As soon as Frankie said the words, he knew they weren't true, look at what he'd done with the bookstore – and in a library, at that.

With one stroke, Paulie pulled out his gun and shot his uncle dead. He wiped his brow, and then knelt down where Frankie's lifeless body laid. He felt around in his pockets and took out his pack of smokes.

After he grieved for a minute, he called Gino and planted a plan to get the girls out of town. Not sure what Melva's rich aunt would do, surely she'd be terrified to say the least … he'd have to make sure all were safe and out of harm's way. Not knowing that Stallinoz was dead, he could not anticipate the reaction to Frankie's death. Paulie knew one thing for sure … he was going back home to see Mamma. Italy. He needed a long vacation before he started making plans for the business side of things and personal decisions with Melva.

And he'd have to get use to a furball. He never considered himself a cat person, but for Melva he'd do *anything* – and that 'anything' would include kissing that cat's ass, no doubt.

Chapter Eighteen

Melva rushed into her condo after telling Gerdy and Gino she'd need time to tidy up a bit before the rendezvous with Paulie. She was so nervous to be on her way to spend more time with her Italian hunk, not to mention meeting his mother. Good god, hope she was ready for a specimen like her. She didn't know squat about this little Italian woman, but from what the cliché's were in all the movies, there would bound to be some friction upon their meeting. However, she was too excited to think about all that right now. She had to get herself and her furry wide-butt feline ready to tote around the globe.

The phone rang. It was Gerdy.

"Now don't get your panties in a wad, but you really shouldn't want to clean right now." She and Gino panicked when Melva mentioned 'tidying up a bit' before she left with Paulie.

"Listen, we are about to be killed and you want to clean your damn place up, for what girl? Whoever's out there will not care if your stove's spotless, they'll just ransack the place and then shoot a bullet in you *and* your precious Brinks!"

She was fuming and a little scared as it dawned on her that yes, this could really happen. Melva wouldn't be able to handle anything so horrible happening to her precious Brinks. Shit!

"Oh, Gerdy, you're just trying to hurry me up."

Gerdy wondered if she was in shock or just out of touch with reality.

"Besides, Auntie Bertha needs to lay down a bit, and I've given her some tea to help her relax. She's been through an ordeal and I must say she's not use to this, Gerdy."

"Melva are you retarded or something?" She resorted to raising her voice. "You. Need. To. Get. Out. Of. Town. Now. Do you understand me? Paulie's waiting!"

"Oh, very well Gerdy, I'll skip the vacuuming, is that okay with you?"

"So, hurry up and get that cat, Bertha, and yourself ready to go. For all we know this complex may not even be standing when and *if* we ever come back."

"Gerdy, Paulie's going to take care of everything, you'll see. So, what are your plans, because if you stay here, I'll worry all the time and won't be able to enjoy myself in whatever part of country I end up. Brinks too, he'll miss his auntie," she giggled nervously. She was terrified. She knew her aunt would be on her private plane to London. But what of Gerdy?

"To tell you the truth, Melva, I need to stay around here. I have the coffee shop to help with, I just can't leave, you know. Maybe Gino has an idea, or Paulie knows where I can stay to be safe for a while. Honestly, I'm not that afraid —you should have seen me with that gun. Girl, I was smokin'!" She snorted proudly. She had plans already.

"I really don't think you should stay around here … maybe you could take a leave of absence, would your terrible boss go for that? Melva answered her own question.

"Really, he doesn't need to know everything that's happening in your life, what is he your father?"

"I dunno, maybe Earl can lend me his back room for a while, I'm not as picky as some as to where I live." She wanted Melva to know that she'd be able to take care of herself.

Melva realized that she might never see her best friend again, "Gerdy?" She sniffled into the phone, "Say you'll be careful and call me all the time, please?"

"Okay, goofy, don't get all mushy on me" … there was a silence between them, "just hurry up and get ready, we'll talk before you leave, just come by on your way out, okay?" Gerdy hung up the phone quickly. She headed over to her bedroom, reached into her nightstand, grabbed two large Hershey bars, and wolfed them down comforted by the chocolate.

Melva helped her frantic aunt pack up five suitcases.

"My dear, I really urge you to think about what you are doing with this character, Paulie. I am nervous, I tell you. I know he's gorgeous, but honestly, looks aren't everything. I know you think he's grand and perfect for you, but what if he turns on you … and I never see my only niece again. What of that?" Terrified she broke down. Her make-up ran down her face making her look like a deranged raccoon.

"Now, now," Melva patted her aunt's hand and sat her down as Brinks looked at both of them as if they were the most boring of creatures. He wanted food, not two women crying. "Sit down by Brinks … see, he'll comfort you, just stroke his fur – it's a great de-stressor, I promise." Brinks bared his teeth at both annoying humans, jumped down, and sashayed toward the kitchen.

She sat down next to her aunt. "Auntie, after all that's happened, I'm sure Paulie didn't save me, only to invite me to go away with him, just to murder me, right?"

"Well, it does seem that he does care for you, but I'm just so nervous. Please keep in touch with me and if you need anything at all, to get away from him – if he's not up to par, of course – then, please telephone me in London and I'll do whatever humanly possible to get you away from him." She quickly reminded her niece of the funds available for her at all times regardless of any circumstances, "You can have whatever you need, I'm only a phone call away … now, how about a spot of tea before I leave?"

Bertha smiled and took a deep breath, she was tired and not use to all the excitement of the younger folks. She longed to be in her own house, enjoying crumpets on her balcony.

After their tea and talk, she called her aunt a limo to zip her to the airport. The quicker Bertha landed in London, the better. She went on sorting through her outfits to take with her and nearly forgot that she had a job, and what of the library?

"Oh crap!" She turned to her furry, and most of the time, grouchy roommate, "Brinks you know what I totally forgot?" He ignored her. "Lomechick —what the hell do I tell her, huh?" She contemplated calling Gerdy for advice, but quickly threw that thought away. "Think, think," she mimicked Winnie the Pooh, one finger tapping the side of her head.

A light bulb went off in her head.

"I'll tell her I've got an incurable disease and have to go live with my aunt in London … Or, I have to go take care of a sick relative indefinitely — yeah, that's it!" She flung clothes across the bed and ran to the kitchen to call Lomechick, but noticed it was going on midnight – she had no choice but to phone Lomechick at home. God help her.

"Who the hell's calling at this hour? Hello?" Mr. Lomechick was not happy.

"Hello, pleasant evening, may I speak to Mrs. Lomechick – just for a brief second, please," she asked politely.

"Who the hell are you, and do you know what hour it is lady!"

"Yes, sir, but I need to speak to her, it's very urgent. I work for her at the library —just for a second, then I'll let you all sleep.

"Why thank you, we wouldn't want to sleep peacefully until you said so …" his voice trailed off as he cursed the very day she was born.

Mrs. Lomechick was just as pissed.

"Melva," she already knew the dingbat was on the other line, "Why in god's name have you called me this late, or do I really want to know?" She signed heavily. Silence came.

"I'm terribly sorry for this phone call, but I wanted to let you know I don't think I'll be able to be at work tomorrow or any day after that … see, I have —"

Lomechick didn't want to hear any more excuses. She was very sleepy and just didn't care one way or another if Melva fell off the face of the earth. "Fine. I'll replace you in the morning." With that, it was all over, no more seeing Lomechick's stern, discontented face.

Melva slowly hung up the phone, her eyes swelled with tears insulted that Lomechick dismissed her so easily. She turned to the feline, who was perched on the back of her vanity chair. "Well, Brinks, I guess that's it then, huh?"

The feline blinked once and then proceeded to lick his paw: All was "right" in his fat-cat- kitty-world.

Chapter Nineteen

News of Stallinoz traveled fast. After waking up alone in the dark hallway, with sore bones from the fall, Big Bones high-tailed it out of town and Gino didn't know where the thug went and he honestly didn't care at the moment. With Nonna throwing a hissy fit about leaving her nice, humble house, while hearing about the Castocci *famiglia* quickly taking over, he was exhausted. He decided to get Nonna squared away at a secret location until the dust died down a bit; he told Paulie to go have fun with his *goumada* in Italy. He doubted very much that anyone would mess with Paulie, after news of him killing off his uncle, a *capo*, got out.

The only thing Paulie and Gino knew was that news of the new don of the Castocci *famiglia* was: Do not screw with this person, in any way shape or form. Now, the news that they had to come to grip with most of all was the rumor that it was a woman – this was an iniquitous idea – which they really could not fathom. A woman 'Boss' was just so preposterous, for anyone to think they could lead a crime family *and* be a woman at the same time, was just not done. Not even in the 21st century.

A don was usually male, late thirties or older, *maybe it was just time for that change to take effect now*. Paulie thought.

Paulie had gathered around Nonna's table to eat a Panini sandwich she had tearfully prepared before Gino forced her to pack.

"Hey Gino, is she gonna cry all freakin' night?"

"Hey-ho Paulie, she's sad, okay? Have some bad news for you, *Compagno* …

"What?" He took a huge bite out of the sandwich. He wanted to pick Melva up, but first wanted Nonna safely gone. "Damn old woman," he mumbled.

He had what could be called a heart-felt moment with her when he tried to hug her after Gino broke the news to her, but Nonna cursed the day he was born and slapped him upside the head with her wet towel.

"Well, my nonna – god bless – her, she's gonna call your mamma to tell her that you threw her outta her own house, this is bad news, eh?" He wanted to giggle, but thought better of it. He knew Paulie's mamma would not be a happy Italian woman when she received that phone call. She'd rip Paulie's balls off!

"What the hell? —She's about to ruin my plans, Gino! Tell her I'm not the one who's throwing her out, blame that shit off on yourself, okay? You know I'm on my way to my mamma's and now I won't have no balls for Melva." He caught Gino's twinkle of laughter in his eyes as they both busted out laughing, just like old times. He finished his last bite and got up to finish packing for his trip back home; he just hoped that his mamma was in a better mood than Gino's nonna was.

Gino stopped Paulie on the way out, "*Compagno*, don't get yourself whacked, since I won't be there to protect you," he tapped his piece that he had hidden in his jacket.

"You do the same … now, get your ass up and get your nonna outta here, *capisce*?" He left before Gino answered.

He would miss his *Compagno*, but he knew that he'd be all right without him for a while. He needed to figure out what to do with his life that was why the trip back to Italy was essential at this time. He wanted to get to know Melva and get use to the furball, Brinks. His drive to be out on his own doing his own businesses began to diminish after he saw how Melva could have been hurt, he didn't know if that was what he wanted to do and with Stallinoz dead, well, maybe this was a sign of some kind. One thing was for sure, he had feelings for someone that he didn't mind putting first before himself.

The fact that he killed his own uncle, which surely would not go over well with his mamma, since this was her brother didn't bother him much … what did, however, was the new don. He couldn't wait to find out who *that* woman was. If it came to whacking a woman boss, then that was what it was.

Chapter Twenty

Melva didn't have time to think about her condo after taking what Gerdy said to heart. She'd like to come back to it someday and perhaps share it with her two favorite males. No doubt about it, she was ready to travel. She had picked out a nice bronze colored top with her favorite Cavariçci jeans and a pair of high-heeled Jimmy Choo sandals to match. She wanted to look sexy for Paulie when he came to whisk her off. No phone call from him yet, but she knew that he probably had things to take care of for himself. She had a talk with Brinks and told him to be on his best kitty-behavior. It had just been spinster and feline for so long this whole relationship thing was new to both.

She went to the closet in her home library where she kept Brinks' kitty carrier. Brinks had not traveled, ever. Still, she hoped he would enjoy the trip.

"Here kitty kitty, come and get in your carrier," hoping the temperamental feline would just jump on in.

"Oh, there you are my sweet boy." She cooed at the grouch, who was perched on one of the barstools in the kitchen – waiting – for kitty crunchies.

She very gingerly scooped up her hefty cat and wrestled him in the carrier, after he had a few claws in her arm first.

"Well, that wasn't so bad, now was it?" she asked the pissed off cat. She put the carrier down, while the contents yowled as if being murdered. She decided the scratches and bite marks were not a pretty sight and could use some antibacterial ointment.

"Great, blooded arms, just great, thanks a lot Brinks." The phone rang.

"Hello?"

"*Goumada*, how's my gorgeous redhead?"

"Oh, hi there, I'm fine, where are you?" She felt all tingly again. She loved this feeling!

"I'll be there soon, then we'll get outta town, okay?" His velvet voice purred.

"I'll be waiting. Oh, Paulie?"

"Yeah?"

"Do we need to buy a ticket for Brinks? I've never flown with him before and I really don't want him without me, you know a mother's concern." She giggled and hoped she didn't sound silly.

"No worries, *goumada*, I've taken care of *everything* … what will you do about your car? Will your friend want it, hate to see that nice ride go to waste parked there, because I'm picking you up in a limo, so be ready."

"How wonderful, a limo? Wow! Uh, not sure about my Mercedes, but maybe Gerdy will take it and drive it while I'm gone, okay?"

"*Ciao Bella*, see you soon." With that, he hung up the phone.
She loved it when he spoke in his native tongue.

Paulie had arranged to have a stretch limo take them to the airport where a private jet waited for them … Melva did not need to worry about her cat, he was set to arrive in Italy in style.

When she arrived at Gerdy's door, Brinks in tow, she was already fighting back tears.

Gerdy yanked the door open and looked as if she had fallen out of bed: Her hair was a mess, favorite robe turned inside out and chocolate ran down her chin.

"What on earth are you doing, Gerdy?" She proceeded to enter the not-so-clean condo.

"Wait!" She blocked Melva with her body.

"What's gotten into you all the sudden?" She was confused with the odd behavior from her best friend. The chocolate running down her chin was nothing new, but all the other things were noticeably different.

"Ummm, place is a mess and I didn't have time to clean up before you graced me with your presence," Gerdy curtsied just for grins, "let's just talk out here, okay?"

"Fine, whatever … kiss your nephew 'cause I really can't say when you two will get together again to cuddle." She managed a smile. She felt something was *not* right about Gerdy, but maybe she was just nervous about the whole trip and being alone with Paulie again.

She tried to object to the kiss. "Do I have to kiss him through the damn metal door? Honestly, Melva the poor thing looks like he's about to die in there – you need to get him a larger cat carrier," all of a sudden, his aunt was concerned.

Leave me alone human or else. Hello! I'm starving in here!

"Okay, just pretend then." Melva didn't want to say good-bye to Gerdy, but she sure was acting as if this was no big deal, leaving her all alone like this. "Oh, before I forget." Melva pulled her key ring out of her purse and placing it in Gerdy's hand, "Keep my Mercedes until I get back, okay?" She genuinely smiled at her best friend ... she'd miss her considerably, more than she'd know.

"Call me when you get wherever Mr. Hotpants takes you, okay? You know I'll worry about the two of you." She smiled and revealed a chocolate covered tooth.

They hugged and then Gerdy – without so much as a good-bye – closed the door. Melva's heart sank. She really didn't expect Gerdy to react this way toward her ... she shrugged it off, "maybe she's just upset that I'm leaving," she told Brinks, and headed down toward the garage area to wait for her Mr. Hotpants.

Paulie was ready to get the hell out of Catswillow, but noted to himself that he'd like to come back and visit from time to time when he needed a quiet place to think. He hoped Melva loved his country and would love his mamma – or the other way around, he tried to think positive either way.

Gino and his nonna left to an undisclosed area; Nonna was eager to go back to Italy also, but Gino convinced her to wait a while longer, then he'd escort her personally back to her old neighborhood. He had legwork to do on information leading to the new lady-boss, so Nonna would have to wait it out ... hidden some place.

"*Compagno*, I'll be in touch," was all he said to Gino as he climbed into the limo.

Brinks had calmed down some, but not entirely. Melva was sure that he needed his daily tuna. She looked down at her marked arms and grimaced. She didn't blame Brinks for being a spoiled brat; after all, it was she who had catered to every kitty-whim. Would Paulie spoil him also —she knew he wouldn't.

Chapter Twenty-one

She wiped an area clean on the bench with a tissue from her purse so she could sit down and waited on her hunk, wondering why it was taking so long. Passing the time, she looked around and glanced at her gorgeous Mercedes parked where she had left it, and it seemed like she had not driven it in a month. She would miss it. She got up and walked toward it and as she neared she fumed, "Damn, a nose print!" She cleaned that up and stepped back to admire her car that she was leaving to her best friend. As she turned back toward the yowling of the cage, she saw the limo Paulie had promised drive up to where she was standing. She couldn't believe how in just a few weeks she had a gorgeous (Mob) boyfriend, been kidnapped, and had quit her job. At the same time, she worried some about her aunt, but knew that the old gal could take care of herself.

He opened the door while the driver stayed put in the driver's seat and motioned her over. His smile melted her from her head to her Jimmy Choo sandals.

"*Goumada*, are you ready?"

"Yes, *we* are." She ran to pick up the carrier where it sat and then ran back to the limo. Out of breath, but excited.

He glided out to let them both in, looked the cage over once, "How's it goin' *gatto*?" He didn't expect the feline to answer, but wanted his *goumada* to know he was making an effort.

She smiled and kissed him on his forehead and hoped that was okay to do.

He planted one right on her lips before she could climb in, "Now that is how you say 'hello' in my language."

They high-tailed it to the airport and boarded a Falcon private jet that could seat nine, it was a beauty, and she was about to experience travel in the fashion of her Aunt Bertha. She could get use to this life.

"Paulie is this yours?" she asked while stepping out of the limo.

"Could be," he grinned ear to ear.

"I know Aunt Bertha has a jet, but I'm not sure if it's quiet as glamorous as this one.

"If you like it, after you've been in it a while, I can buy it for you; it doesn't have a bed, but it's got a large counter space," he nodded wickedly. He was use to jetting around with his uncle and having business meetings with Stallinoz, when he was alive.

She stared up at him in amazement, "You'd do that for me?"

"*Goumada*, I'd kill for you." He said this with every honest meaning. She did not doubt this …

The three of them boarded with not so much as a 'meow' from Brinks —it just might be a great trip after all!

While Melva, Paulie and Brinks were on their way to the airport, a full-recovered Big Bones was awaiting orders. "Have we secured a meeting place?" The female asked the man on the other end of the line.

"We have."

"No screw-ups, Carparillini, got that?"

"Big Bones is there and ready for his assignment."

"No assignments yet, let them get settled in Italy, it's not like we don't know where they've gone." The female's voice was firm and confident.

Carparillini's female boss knew systematically what she wanted to do, but he was still getting use to having a female don. Nonetheless, he knew she was powerful and had backing of the Castocci *famiglia*, they had waited a long time for her to rise to power.

With a light sense of humor, he asked, "Have you thought about what you wanna be called: don, boss, or donna?" Carparillini asked his new boss and hoped she chose one by now.

"Nah, just call me Miss 'C' I kinda like the way that sounds."

"It's customary to address the head of the *famiglia* as 'Godfather,' maybe you should think about something other than Miss 'C,' ya know?"

"When I want your two cents I'll ask for it, I've made up my mind, deal with it." She hung up the phone; she was a busy woman now.

Chapter Twenty-two

Several hours later and jetlag running through her body, Melva was relieved to land and her pussycat was just as thrilled. She had let Brinks roam about the cabin, without any objections from any of the pilots, or Paulie. She was too busy playing tongue hockey with her Italian stallion to pay attention to her cat investigating the jet.

He wanted to take her in mid-flight, on that counter he mentioned earlier, in front of all to see, but thought better of it since he wanted to play the perfect gentleman and drive her crazy with his kisses. He did manage a small hickey at the base of her neck so all could see she was 'marked.'

She had never received a hickey, ever! She was so horny she could barely contain herself, and she was about to meet her (no doubt in her mind) future mother-in-law. *What would she think of me?* She had full confidence that she would make a wonderful first impression.

As the jet landed, Paulie had managed to get Brinks in the carrier without any resistance or any type of body injury. She wondered how Paulie did that. He was a very brave man.

"*Goumada*, the pussy's in the cage, ready?" He smirked and winked at her. She was so gorgeous with her tousled hair, due to their make-out session.

"I think so – to be honest – I'm very nervous, and I look like such a mess. I wanted to look nice for your family. Do you think they'll approve?"

"No worries, *goumada*, we are stopping some place where you can get yourself all dolled up, okay?" He took the cat carrier and proceeded out the door, which the pilots opened for them. All they did was bow at him as if he were the king of Saudi Arabia.

There at Rome's international airport was another limo parked in front of the doorway to pick them up. He had taken care of everything, in Italy, too.

Melva was happiest she'd ever been and it only seemed to get better. She sniffed in the wonderful European air. She noticed tour buses and tiny cars everywhere that sat only two; this was very different since rarely seen in the States. She wondered if these cute little cars would ever catch on across the Atlantic, and knew Gerdy would like one.

She patted him on the shoulder, (and loved the way that felt under her fingers tips), "Those little cars are called what?"

He looked around and spotted one, "Those are Smart Cars, you like?"

"Yeah, they are cute, but not for me, for Gerdy … I think she'd like one."

"Maybe you can send her one, she'll be happy to drive one around Catswillow, 'm sure of that." He motioned to the limo driver to open the door for her and her cat. He instructed in Italian where they needed to go. She loved to listen to him talk.

Melva looked around and tried to absorb the surroundings of her first sights of taly, even though it was only the airport, she could see Italians from all lifestyles. One man was holding his small dog, perhaps waiting on a girlfriend or family member; another Italian man held up a sign for someone named "Connor," perhaps an American executive. She knew this much: She was lucky, driven around Italy in a limo opposed to a tour bus!

After sitting in traffic for a bit, they finally reached their hotel.

Melva gasped at the sight of the beautiful, posh hotel.

A few men scrambled to open the doors to the limo, and took their luggage out of the truck. Without asking, they just did.

"*Buongiorno*!" A handsome man addressed her.

"Oh, hello there," and placed Brinks' carrier in his hand that he extended out toward her.

"Thank you very much, sir," she said to the young man and proceeded to enter the fabulous hotel.

Paulie dismissed the driver and followed her into the lounge area. The eager manager met them.

Paulie and the manager kissed each other on the cheek, from what she gathered they had known each other a long time. It was nice to see him in his own country with acquaintances and friends.

Melva looked around the hotel to check out how clean it was. It was immaculate and she loved how the luminous of the lighting made everything so romantic.

Paulie waved to her to come closer. Brinks was a good boy, no yowling for at least ten minutes, she wondered if he had passed out on her from lack of tuna. She checked him out and cooed at him. Brinks merely hissed, so she knew he was good as gold.

"I want you to meet an old friend of my *famiglia*, Agostino, he's the owner."

"*Bella, magnifico!*" Agostino hugged her before she could place Brinks down.

"Agostino, her cat – in the cage – have you got food for him?" His caring gesture melted her inside. She loved this man! Did Brinks love him too? But, knowing her cat he most likely had not yet made up his little mind.

Agostino knelt down to see the ample cat, still as a statue, staring back at him.

"I believe we just may have some fish left over from our dinner hour, I'll check for you."

He went off, located one of his servers from the kitchen and returned with great news. "My busboy will bring something up to your suite for him and you, if you'd like some supper, no?"

She was ravenous and agreed that would be great.

She loved Rome, Roma, as the Italians referred. She noticed the fancy boutique and stopped to take a look-see.

"*Goumada*, you want to shop?" He squeezed her hand. He wanted to squeeze everything on her!

"Maybe later," she really wanted to check out her suite first and shower, or take a long, hot bath …*Would he join me?* —She prayed he would.

"You can do whatever you want, *goumada*, just say the word, *capisce?*" He kissed her forehead and took the heavy carrier from her hand.

She didn't want anyone else to carry Brinks, since he was around strangers and strange surroundings.

They stopped at one door and Agostino opened it and stood aside while he gestured to her to go in.

"Hope that this is to the *signora's* liking?" He smiled and walked in behind her.

She looked around in awe; she had only seen this kind of luxury in magazines. Tapestries lined the windows, the carpet was a soft tone gold and bronze and the bed was dark cherry wood dressed in satin sheets. She pictured him right smack in the middle of all that with her on top! *Brinks would have to find himself some other room to occupy.* She giggled to herself at that very thought.

"Paulie, your room is joined here," Agostino went through one door located near the bathroom. "Both of you enjoy your stay and the supper will be right up, *buonasera*." As he left her room, he placed the key on the dresser for her.

She proceeded to unhook Brinks' cage to let the poor thing out and about. A feline cooped up wasn't a pretty sight. He ran off and then jumped on 'his' bed, and started licking his behind. "There, that's more like it," she chimed. He was content.

Paulie started walking toward his door, "I'll be back soon, relax a little while."

Chapter Twenty-three

She had no chance to object or say, anything … he was out the door fast.

"Well, that was quick … maybe I'll just straighten up a bit," she stopped herself from opening a drawer next to the bed and wondered how Aunt Bertha, Gerdy and Paulie's friend, Gino were doing. She was certain that her aunt was – by now – enjoying her tea out on her balcony … she hoped Gerdy was in a better mood by now. She thought of calling Gerdy, but thought better of it. "I'll call in a few more days and give her a full report."

While she was in Italy, maybe she'd take a train to Paris, then on to visit her aunt in England, spend some time with her and take in the fresh air, at her countryside mansion. She didn't think Paulie would care, besides he was a businessman, was he not? He would probably like that time to take care of whatever things needed doing. She grew excited with the thought of seeing her aunt and shopping! Some of her Jimmy Choo's looked worn out a bit anyway.

After what seemed a lifetime, he popped back over as promised.

She had managed to dust off the desk area, with tissues she found in the bathroom, fluff her pillow, and slip into some stretch Capri pants and a snug tee shirt just in time for his return.

"I'm in here," she yelled back to him that she was in the bathroom. She wanted that hot bath, but wasn't sure if she'd get her wish tonight. She thought about sleep for a second and realized she hadn't slept in a good day. *Time flies by when you're with a hunk of a man!*

He found her bent over against the lavatory countertop; she was checking out her make-up, but he really wasn't looking at her face …

"*Goumada* …" he purred and slipped behind her. He wanted to be inside her. Now.

She reached for him while she faced the mirror; she guided his masculine hand up her thigh.

Someone knocked on the door.

"*Maledizione*, must be the supper," he cursed and then left her there wanting more…

"Shit!" She was tired of interruptions.

The server walked in after he led him into the suite. The server then showed him the spread of food for them and then lifted the silver tray cover to reveal, what Paulie thought was the main course, it was not, it was a knife. They struggled and she peeked around the door to see what all the commotion was about and saw that they were making a mess of things.

Oh god where was Brinks?! She panicked and picked up the first thing she saw back in the bathroom, a blow dryer.

She dashed over toward the two men and hit the server right over the head with it. The blow dryer shattered into tiny pieces and the server tumbled to the ground.

"Good job, *Goumada,*" Paulie managed to say after catching his breath. "What the hell was this all about?" He felt it may have been a warning from the *Castocci brogata,* but how would they know about him being here … exactly at *this* hotel?

He was going to find out, but first he'd get rid of the body. The server wasn't dead, he knew that whoever sent him here would try again, maybe not with this same man, but someone and he didn't want her or the cat hurt in any way. How would he turn his life around with so many disturbances? He guessed he'd have to take care of loose ends and prove that he wasn't into taking part of killings any longer. He had too much to lose now.

"Are you all right, *Goumada?*" He stepped closer to her and hugged her.

"Yes, I'm okay, but where's my Brinks?" She panicked and then kicked the man lying on the floor for scaring her cat into hiding. "Brinks, where are you. Here kitty, got fish for you, come on Brinks come out!" She knelt down to look under the king sized bed while Paulie took the man and placed him out on the balcony ledge, one wrong move and the man would surely tumble to his death. However, he didn't kill him, that's what was important.

Brinks was located at the very top of the bed directly under the headboard. He was not a happy kitty-camper.

She crawled under the bed the best she could, grabbed his furry arm, and brought him out to safety. She kissed his furry face and Brinks wanted down. "There now, all's better with Mamma's little boy."

"We need to leave." Paulie said as he locked the suite's door. "As fast as you can get ready, it's not safe here." He took her arm and kissed her hand, "We'll be okay someplace else, I'll be right back." He went to his room and closed the door.

She began her re-packing, but first she did what she promised and fed Brinks his fish. She placed more in the carrier so that he'd jump right in when it was time to go. Brinks did not jump. *Woman let me eat; a hungry cat is a death wish.*

When Paulie came back into the room, he found her on the floor picking up pieces from the blow dryer she used to save him. Brinks was sitting on the bed supervising her project.

"*Goumada*, are you ready?" He reached for Brinks, who did not resist his strong grip and led him into his carrier.

"Wow, how did you do that? With me he causes such a battle."

"I dunno, maybe it's because we both are guys, we have an understanding …" Paulie grinned and hoped Brinks behaved at his mamma's house, because that's where they were heading.

They quickly took the elevator down to the garage parking lot, where again, a driver waited on them. But, this was a Mercedes sedan, not a fancy limo.

They settled in the sedan and whisked off towards *Firenze,* Florence.

"Where are we heading?" She was so tired and just wanted some rest. She laid her head on his shoulders and tried to fight the inevitable sleep.

"Rest a bit, *Goumada*; we are going to my *famiglia's* house in *Firenze*...Florence.

"Florence? Really? I've always thought that to be a beautiful area, well … the books at the library had awesome pictures, which were of that part of Italy."

"Well, you'll see it now, up close. You'll love it there, I'm sorry that you didn't see *Roma* as I had wished, but you'll see *Firenze* and *Naples*, okay?" He winked at her and she knew he was good on that promise. First, she wanted sleep.

Brinks had meowed until she let him out so that he could stretch out on their laps; Paulie didn't mind so much, after the long trip and then someone trying to kill him, this was nothing. The furball had better not make a habit of it though.

He had told the driver to stop a local café so that he could purchase something for them to tie them over until morning. He hoped his mamma would make a delicious breakfast on his behalf.

They ate the small snack, kissed each other, and then closed their eyes a bit – it was a short drive – but even the smallest of meals and naps were welcomed.

Chapter Twenty-four

Carparillini cracked his knuckles; he was in a foul mood after the news that one of his soldiers was dead, he was supposed to send Paulie a little message, but the idiot fell to his death, from what Carparillini could tell was this soldier could not even carry out this small task. His only goal was to plant a fright into Paulie and his woman, keep them on the move, that's all. Carparillini didn't know how the lady-boss would take the news, but with any luck, she wasn't going to be a bitch about it. He should have taken care of Paulie after he took care of Stallinoz. This big mess was taking up time he didn't have. Pressure from his lady-boss to keep Paulie running, and not just killing the bastard, was beyond his comprehension. All he knew was she didn't exactly want them hurt. Yet. He didn't want his ass thrown off a bridge so he did what she asked of him.

Carparillini entered a large room. He noticed most of the faces seated at the table, but a few were ones who came over – after a bit of persuasion from the takeover – and the murder of Stallinoz.

The new *consigliere* was the lady-boss's cousin, all in the *famiglia*, that's how it was. Big Bones stared at his scar that Stallinoz had given him the day of his death. Big Bones cursed, "Bastard." He had been through hell most of his childhood, grew up with the labels, he demanded some respect now. His cousin was a pain in his ass, but being *famiglia* you just put up with it.

Miss C. got up from her comfortable zebra printed chair, "Was the message delivered to Paulie and Melva?" She looked around, at what she thought were the most pathetic of an organization, just because they were all men. Besides, she had cramps. She figured she would blame all the men for her sour mood.

Big Bones, her cousin, started to speak, "nah, dumb-ass bastard didn't do as he was told, got himself killed," Big Bones snorted awkwardly.

"Shut-up or get lost today. I'm in no mood for screw-ups from any of you, got it?" She eyed each one to challenge her, knowing she really could use someone with some wisdom.

She remembered her father and how he always told her she would reach this point in her life, and told her he'd watch over her from above. She remembered her life and her friends, some she missed, but knew that they had moved on just as she did. Her own life had been lies, even as a child, but it was all to protect her until adulthood and the takeover of the business, which was inevitable. She would do her best to profit and to rule, just as her father did. She learned from the most important men in her life, that she was the only one who could carry out their legacy, even though most of it was illegal — but they would be proud of her accomplishments.

Her cousin was an idiot that is why he wasn't the boss.

"I don't get why we play cat and mouse with these two, and where is Gino? I'm sure he can be persuaded to do work for us." A man directly under Carparillini's directive asked Miss C.

"Carparillini, your man doesn't have complete confidence in me, why is that you think?" She stared at the two men.

"*Per favore*, with all respect, he does not understand the importance of the situation, yet," Carparillini continued, "we are all a little confused on why you want them alive, may we all know now?" He hoped she wouldn't blast his ass away in front of everyone. Her father would not have thought twice about doing that.

"*Capisco*, I can understand why this must be important for all of you to know. Know this: Frankie left many businesses out there for the taking, and Paulie, I doubt, will not let those businesses fade; our *famiglia* will be those who take it. We go after the ones in Italy first. I have no doubts that Paulie will try to make those legit, but I'm not interested in legit, only making all of Stallinoz' dealings ours now. As you know, those were started by Stallinoz himself."

The lady-boss knew that she wanted the nice, large, profitable shipping business near Florence; a tip led her to Paulie continuing his journey there, so this was perfect. As for Gino, she knew that he would eventually speak to Paulie of his plans. She had men planted all around Italy, and knew Gino would show up in the near future to help Paulie.

Melva was another story, if she got in her way … then, that would be the end of Paulie's *Goumada*. In her business, there wasn't time for warm, fuzzy feelings toward a couple in love.

"What's our next move?" Big Bones asked anyone who would listen to him for a change.

His lady-boss cousin turned to face him, "I want you to head out to Italy and find us a location which isn't a 'hot place,' let Carparillini know when that's secure and I'll let you know when I'll be out there. Leave Paulie and Melva to me. Go." With that, she left the room full of testosterone and headed to her dining area she was famished!

Chapter Twenty-five

Paulie nudged Melva and Brinks, who was on his lap, to wake up. They were driving up to the house his parents have lived in since they were married.

Brinks hated someone waking him up from a relaxing nap, so he took his sweet feline time and stretched this way and that, finally licking his lips and gingerly jumped in the carrier Paulie had opened for him. Melva wasn't surprised at Brinks for being so cooperative toward his soon-to-be dad. She grinned at the thought of it all.

He kissed Melva on the forehead and squeezed her soft hand, "*Goumada* we are here at last, it's late so we will be very quiet, *capisce*?" He bid the driver farewell in Italian.

She couldn't believe how beautiful the house was, something out of a dream. The modest, vine-lined home stood between other houses, but this one had iron accents that gave the home a truly European feel. The house was in the center of town, but hidden from all the shops and cafés that tourists would most likely be occupying. The cobblestone road reminded her of the library books' pictures that she had told Paulie about earlier. It stood, from what onlookers could see, on three stories; two balconies extend out for one to sit and read, or just enjoy the gorgeous view.

It was very quiet around the neighborhood, but then again it was in the middle of the night.

She grew more excited just standing there watching Paulie staring at his home, hoping he felt relieved and happy to be home. She guessed that was why he looked so at peace. His handsome face was more relaxed now than before. She knew he had a lot on his mind and she knew that she'd do whatever to please him. As she thought about it, in the back of her mind, the scary feeling of meeting his mamma was frightening. She felt a lump in her throat. She wished the woman would pop out and say hello or something. She looked around at the iron-gated doors and thought those were pretty well kept and clean. She knew it would not be good to judge this Italian woman's cleaning. Oh, but she hoped she had a tidy bathroom for her.

She tried to make herself presentable and asked Paulie, "Do you think I'll get to meet your mother right now?" She smiled nervously; she knew it was a long shot.

"*Goumada*, they might be asleep, it's very late. But, let's go in if you and your cat are ready." He opened the iron-gated doors and let her and Brinks pass into the gardened front area.

Brinks started meowing at just the precise time that the door flew open.

Melva's heart started to race, right out of her chest.

"*Santo Cielo! No gatto!*" Paulie's mamma freaked at the sight of Brinks in his carrier.

"Mamma no!" He tried to stop the Italian powerhouse.

"What the hell is she doing with my cat?" She rushed in not waiting to see Paulie's reaction, and followed the woman out onto the first balcony.

Paulie watched in horror as the two went back and forth in two different languages.

"*Mamma! Basta!* That is enough leave the *gatto* alone." He jerked the kitty carrier out of her grasp.

There on the balcony sat poor Brinks yowling, in the carrier, his kitty-world had flashed before his eyes. *Tuna woman! I need tuna, now!*

"*This was going to be an exciting visit,*" Melva thought.

After his two women calmed down, a bit, so that he could put two words in, he sat his mamma down on her wooden bench in her small kitchen. His father stepped in as he did this.

"My son, how are you? Good to see you, you're mamma has missed you terribly," his father sounded so happy his son was home, he didn't even notice his wife's ruffled feathers.

"Papa, sorry we woke you up, are you doing all right?" He knew his father wasn't in the best of health after his last birthday.

"*Grazie, grazie*, my son … I am okay, I think," he pointed to the Italian woman, on the bench, who had pursed lips, "she tells me I'm okay, so I guess I am. He chuckled and Paulie stalwartly hugged him.

His father eyed Melva and grinned, his son had brought home a nice one.

"And this is?" His father went toward her.

Melva kept turning her head, to check out the balcony, that her cat had not croaked in the cage that held him prisoner.

Paulie stood beside her and patted her on the waist; he wanted her to know all would be all right, eventually.

"This is Melva. Melva Klick." He slightly pushed Melva toward his father expecting her to hug the man. Maybe they would hit it off.

"Melva, this is my papa, Marcello, and my mamma, Ermelinda. I'm sure that they are both happy to meet you." He eyed his father and nodded his head, hoping his father took the hint to get his wife to acknowledge his new girlfriend.

"Yes, this is good, no? We will have company, Ermelinda, is this not nice?" Marcello sure hoped his wife would say something, anything at all.

She did.

"No, no, *gatto*. They stink. I cannot clean after the *gatto*; I'm too old for this."

"Mamma, please be patient, Brinks—"

"Brinks?" His mamma slowly repeated the feline's name. "Is he smelly?" she answered her own question, "No smelly *gatto* here!"

"Mamma, once you know him you will like him, *per favore* Mamma, welcome both of them … for me." He smiled at the petite woman and melted her heart. She would die for this man.

Melva's mind was in a panic, wondering if this woman would let Brinks stay inside with her. Her cat was an indoor cat! She liked the dad. She wondered if Paulie would look like this when he was that age. He was still handsome, no doubt about it.

While Paulie spoke to his mother in Italian, she decided she'd wonder around the small living area, connected to the dining room. Everything was so authentic and for being a small, confined area (from what she was use to back home) it was very luxurious. It seemed to her they did have money, or her good son had been sending some major funds. Nonetheless, she loved it. She hope she could stay … and her cat, too.

He came over to where she was standing, "she will hug you now," he led her toward the petite woman and waited for one of them to make the first move. It was late and he wanted some much-needed rest.

She stumbled awkwardly and then extended her hand, "Nice to meet you Mrs. Palazollo." The woman didn't blink, 'sort of like Brinks when he's eyeing the last morsel of tuna,' she observed.

"Nice to meet you, too Melva, our home is your home." It wasn't exactly 'cold' but not exactly a 'warm fuzzy' welcome either.

Melva took it either way. Anything was better than Brinks having to sleep outside in a foreign country.

"Is it all right for my … how do you say … *gatto*, to come in now?"

Paulie and his father chuckled. "You may bring him in and let him out." Marcello said confidently.

His wife's expression told everyone she was not ready for the *gatto* to invade her nice, charming home.

Chapter Twenty-six

The next morning, Melva woke to marvelous aromas filling her small quarters. She was so terribly exhausted from all the traveling, and the small dispute in the middle of the night with Paulie's mother, that she really didn't feel like rearranging the area to her liking. She thought she'd do that today instead, after a home cooked breakfast, of course. She stretched and took in more of the aromas and thought she should get up and move around, and locate her feline, who had not bothered to present himself after she let him out of the carrier. All Brinks wanted to do was crouch low to the ground and find a nice hiding spot.

After she twisted her long auburn hair in up close to her head, she decided to wear something comfortable, "No heels today." She didn't really know what Paulie had planned, but hopefully she could just wear kitten-heeled shoes and still look gorgeous for him. She looked around the small bedroom, she thought it looked as if it were a bathroom at another time; perhaps they did remodel, but she liked it just as it was. She would add her touches here and there and she loved the tiny adjoining bathroom of her own. The bathroom had a nice antique, claw-foot tub and a gorgeous levorotary, that was a nice soft pink hue.

Just as she peeked out of the doorway, Paulie was there to greet his *Goumada*; it seemed an eternity since he'd seen her.

"*Buongiorno Goumada*," he purred in her ear.

"Oh, hi there, did you sleep well?" She wanted to take him into the room and forget about breakfast, but her stomach reminded her that wasn't going to happen. She just couldn't get enough of her delicious hunk.

"Everything smells wonderful," she chimed as she approached Ermelinda near the stove. "Has anyone seen Brinks this morning, he usually sleeps with me, but I didn't feel him at all in the bed."

Ermelinda's eyebrow rose, she wasn't use to cats sleeping in one's bed as a person would, this was new to her. She turned back to her *pancetta* and whispered to herself in Italian.

Melva knew it was probably about what she had said – it was just so different here, but she'd have to make the woman take to her and her cat – she just had to!

Paulie kissed his mother and then his father, who was already sitting down at the wooden table reading the Italian paper. "Melva, your *gatto* was with me when I woke up to walk down to get my newspaper, he is a nice *gatto*.

They all looked over at Brinks, who was licking his ample bottom, on what looked like a very comfortable chair. *People can't you see I'm busy. Where's the tuna?*

She charged at her busy cat and planted a kiss right on the lips that had just licked his rear.

Paulie's mother was mortified … his father didn't seem to mind.

She picked up her cat and hugged him hard. She loved to inhale his kitty-smells.

"Did you miss me, Brinks? You know Mommy likes it when you sleep next to her," she cooed a little more then realized everyone was staring at her. Besides Brinks wanted down, like *now*.

The food, laid out in a nice spread, looked delicious. Marcello said grace and then they were all ready to eat the bountiful breakfast the woman of the house prepared.

Paulie noticed Melva wouldn't 'dig right in' and wondered why. "Do you not like what you see, it's very good, try something." He stared at his mother, the awesome cook, and hoped she didn't get pissed off about Melva eyeing the food as it were going to bite her.

"Um, what's that exactly?" She pointed to a bread-like spread.

"That's very delicious; it's *animelle in pangrattato con canciofi*, breaded sweetbread with artichokes —you will love it, I promise." He waited for his girlfriend to dive right in.

She did not.

She reached for some, all eyes on her, and placed some on her plate. She took a small bite of it … and didn't really care for it, but managed to swallow and smile at the stern-faced cook. "*Grazie*, it's very good."

They all ate, had some small talk about Paulie's adventures as a boy, how he followed his Uncle Frankie around and wanted to go where he went. His parents knew what Paulie and Frankie were into, but Ermelinda never trusted her own brother, Frankie, and that tension never really escaped the *famiglia* where Frankie was concerned. But, she need not worry about her brother any longer; Paulie just had to find the right moment to tell her of his death. Since he died in America, news of that wouldn't come until a good week he knew of that much. If he didn't tell her, then someone in the immediate *famiglia* would, he wanted to be the one to break the news to her.

Marcello raised his head from the half-empty plate, "Where are you two going today? I think you should take her around, get to know the locals. How long will you stay with us?"

She placed her fork down and looked at Paulie, because she didn't really know how long her and Brinks were welcome here. She hoped to stay a good while, besides that, she couldn't stand the thought of being in America while he was over here, thousands of miles away. She suddenly came to the realization that they never discussed their relationship, his business dealings, or really anything for that matter. She wondered when he would bring up these things. She knew he wanted her, but there were interruptions when they were so close to consummating their relationship, every single time.

"Oooh, I would love to have a cappuccino in a local café, maybe one that's your favorite —that would be great!" She grew more excited each minute. She had not even sipped a café mocha, in what seemed like ages ago. She thought briefly about Gerdy … she missed her best friend terribly. She'd have to call her soon.

"Papa, that's a great idea, but soon I'll have to leave Melva and Brinks in your hands, okay? There is much to do … and Mamma, I need to speak with you soon, *per favore?*"

His mother nodded her head and kept eating her scrumptious breakfast. Melva had no idea Paulie was leaving.

"Are you going away?" Her heart sank for a few minutes, but then realized this might be the perfect opportunity to hop on the Euro train and see her aunt. She knew of the nice transit systems Europe offered. Aunt Bertha often spoke of transportation options all around Europe, just in case one day –such as this – Melva would travel out and about Europe.

"Not really, just local stuff, but you might get bored," he remembered at that moment her aunt lived in London some place. "Why not visit your nice aunt, it's not that far, *Goumada*, what do you think?" He really didn't want her anywhere near this area if things were to get ugly; he wasn't for sure if they would, but just in case, she and her cat should leave.

"Oh my god!" She couldn't believe how they thought the same thing.

Ermelinda crossed herself at the mention of her savior.

"I was just thinking of telling you I may go visit my aunt – I can't believe you thought of that – I think I will."

"Good idea then."

Paulie's mamma interrupted their two-way conversation. "Paulie, *figlio*, son, will she take the *gatto*?" His mamma was hopeful, because she noticed fur was accumulating around what had become his 'favorite feline spot.' Ermelinda said a silent prayer.

Melva giggled, "Why of course, he goes where I go, so please do not worry, we'll be back."

Ermelinda glared at everyone and then signed heavily. Then she proceeded to clean up, Melva quickly followed.

"Please let me do this, I love to wash dishes," she turned to Paulie, "please tell her I can do this for her."

"Mamma, *per favore*, let Melva help, you rest with Papa."

With a little opposition, then showing Melva how to use the dishtowel and place her dishes on a rack, she finally sat down in her living room, each time glancing back to see if Melva was screwing up her kitchen.

Brinks, the very brave cat, hopped onto the lap of his death … the vibe he got from the old woman was a good vibe, perhaps it was a mislead vibe. It was a death wish.

She jumped up as if electrocuted and tossed Brinks right on his fat butt and ran out of the room. All they heard was a blaring 'meow' and a door slam.

Chapter Twenty-seven

After the fiasco in the kitchen, they walked hand in hand down the cobblestone alley; soon greeted by Florence's busy *piazza*. There was a café to the right; it was like something out of a romantic movie. To Melva it was just so surreal —that she was here and her gorgeous boyfriend was beside her.

They walked up to the doors of the café, he told her to sit out on the bistro-style table area and he'd bring out their cappuccinos. The air was crisp and clean, not like a busy, smoky street back in America. She wished Brinks could see this, but then again his new grandfather was comforting him. 'Brinks would like the smell of the food circling around the area,' she thought. She knew he'd fit in a carrier with wheels she'd seen once in a magazine; it was quite nice, because it had a screen that would protect him and he could see out, maybe next time she'd bring him.

Paulie walked out with two cups and two biscotti, it all looked so wonderful, and she couldn't stand how excited she was.

"I love you!" she said it before he could place the cups down. He looked at her in a way she'd never seen him look at her before.

She panicked and thought maybe that she should take it back? *Idiot! Don't scare him off.*

"*Goumada*, I love you too," he smiled and kissed her on the lips, softly.

She wanted to scream to the finely carved statues amongst the *piazza*, that she loved him, knowing that – if she did – the statues would probably come to life and applaud her for saying it. Romance was abundantly in the air …

They sat quietly and stared at each other for a bit, and then her nervousness got in the way of things. She started inspecting the small table, arranging its salt and sugar contents, this was not good.

"You don't have to do that you know," he guessed she was nervous, but from what, he didn't really know. Maybe he had it in him to make her this way.

She fumbled and sat up straight and cleared her throat, "Does this area have any nice shops, to buy shoes?"

He looked at her as if she were crazy. "Of course, Italy has shops, fantastic shops." He loved her innocence. "*Goumada*, there's a shop on every corner, take your pick, or go to all of them, I don't mind. Do you not want to just sit and talk for a few minutes? I think we should discuss a little subject ... like my business. You've never asked me anything, why?" He was curious, or maybe she didn't care.

"Oh, Paulie, I'm sorry —it's just that I didn't think you wanted me to pry, guess I was wrong?" She felt a little relieved that he brought up the topic. After all, he had killed his own uncle and lord knows whom else before she even met him. But, for some odd reason, she did not fear him at all. Something about his eyes ...

"I don't ever want you to be afraid to ask me anything, *capisce*? I want you to know everything, because I'm not living my life the way I use to, before I met you. I cannot do this anymore." He wanted as close to a normal life as possible for them. Even for his best *Compagno*, Gino, who he missed terribly.

"I think this is wonderful; we shouldn't hide anything then, so go ahead let it rip." She placed her elbows on the table and leaned closer to him.

"I need you to go stay with your aunt for a while. I need to get one of the largest shipping businesses my uncle had and make it legit, *capisce*, this way we don't worry about nothin' ever." He knew that the Castocci *famiglia* would want it but he'd make sure they didn't get it.

"That's not a problem, Paulie, I can leave soon. I have to call her first to let her know, but I don't mind, it'll be nice to see my aunt. She has a beautiful mansion outside of London you'd love it."

"I'm sure I would," he took her hand and kissed it and noticed Melva never wore rings, just bracelets. He'd have to change that for sure. He smiled at his small secret.

"What?" She smiled back not knowing what he was up to, but he looked as if he were up to something.

"Let's walk around the *piazza* a while. I want you to see some beautiful places here, then we can have lunch at this place I know you'll like, okay my *Goumada*?"

"Yes, let's go ... oh, don't forget, I want shoes too!" She was spoiled, she must say that about herself, but she loved this place.

Gerdy would kill her if she heard her wanting shoes instead of sex. She wanted to call her friend today.

Paulie pointed everything out, even though, at this time, the replica of David was in the process of cleaning and maintenance, it was truly a moving experience for her.

She'd never forget her first sights of David, and then of Perseus holding Medusa's head, she was in awe the whole time —she was lost for words.

He didn't forget that his woman wanted shoes, but wanted to show her the breathtaking Duomo and Campanile tower first.

They walked down the narrow pathway chatting about this and that along the way, when they came upon the tower he literally held her up.

"It's breathtaking is it not, *Goumada*?" He watched how her eyes danced about trying to take in every inch of the tower and surrounding Facade of the Duomo.

She held her hands to her mouth, "I don't know what to say, it's absolutely divine! How do you all live here with such beauty? I just can't believe something like this exists." She turned to look at her beloved.

"We just do, *Goumada*, we just do."
A group of young girls around thirteen at the most, pasted them by and congregated around the Duomo as if it held no history or importance.

She could not fathom this … it was something she felt a connection towards already. This is where she knew that she loved Paulie – no doubts – and no reservations whatsoever. She knew he felt the same, well, after today of course when he said he loved her. She smiled with that thought and she noticed something else: She felt safe there in Florence. If she wished to go off alone to shop or any place, she felt she could do that, too!

As promised, he showed her where a wonderful shop was, encouraging her to buy those shoes that she desired. 'Nothing beat a pair of authentic Italian shoes, nothing,' she mused.

She didn't want this day to end, ever … but she wanted to see her kitty. She was certain he must be so grouchy by now since there was no one to feed, water, or play with him. She prayed that his father had at least given Brinks water. She'd soon find out.

Surely, his mother would have known to feed him something. She felt terrible that she didn't at least have Paulie call once; he did have his cell phone with him all the time she noticed.

After she bought shoes, which were so gorgeous she couldn't wait to show her aunt – who would be green with envy – they headed toward a quant, little restaurant that he said the Calamari was to die for. She took his word, but doubted she wanted any; she'd leave squid-tasting to Gerdy.

Paulie, trained to notice people following him, had a gut feeling to keep his guard up, he was pissed that someone was "clocking" *him*! He knew that these were Castocci soldiers. He had no idea how many, but they were like scorpions, traveling in pairs. He kept his attitude toward Melva happy and interesting; the last thing he wanted was for her to panic. Besides, he knew she'd be busy trying to clean the table up before their meal arrived. He was truly figuring his woman out. Let her clean, what the hell —didn't hurt anybody, his mamma was the same way.

He wanted to get back home, where it was secure enough so that he could call Gino, find out where he was at, and get a plan started as soon as possible. He hoped she would get out of *Firenze* soon, if he told her to, she would.

Dinner was superb, even though she didn't take a bite out of the Calamari Paulie ordered. Nonetheless, her pasta was delicious. She asked for another cappuccino and sipped that with pure delight, she wanted to be blunt with Paulie about when they would have time for sex or a heavy duty make out session like on the plane, but thought better of it since his mind was obviously elsewhere.

Did he want her as much as she wanted him? She wondered over dessert.

Of course he did. His body ached for this woman with fiery red hair and piercing golden eyes, but now was not the time, and his parents' home was defiantly not the place.

He thought about that ring he wanted to get her, he knew just where to go for that extravagant piece of jewelry. He knew people and knew their quality was unbeatable. He just needed the right time to get it and present it to her. He wanted his businesses settled and did not want any trouble from any of Castocci's men or any other *famiglia*, he knew there were other *famiglia's* out there, but Castocci *brogata* was the one he worried about the most.

Chapter Twenty-eight

They arrived at the house to find Brinks sitting smack in the middle of the table, but where were Paulie's parents.

Melva panicked. *Maybe Brinks killed them with his nastiness, is that possible?* She wondered. *That's so ridiculous, I've never heard of a cat killing a human.* She giggled at the thought.

"Mamma, Papa, are you home?" Paulie began to search the house in a panic. He knew men were after him who was capable of doing anything they wanted once they found out where he was staying. He would kill anyone who hurt his parents, he didn't care who they were.

Melva picked up her furry, grouchy feline and placed him on the floor, "you must be so hungry," she glanced at the empty bowel she had placed next to the door. She put down a bowel full of kitty crunchies for him to eat, but he wasn't going for plain, boring food anymore, no way! She guessed by his uninterested look that he wanted something fresh, like fish. Brinks didn't care that eating rich food every day wasn't good for him.

"Fine, Brinks, I'll look and see what Ermelinda has here for you."

While Brinks supervised his mother, Paulie went around the house looking for his parents. Melva fed her darling then joined Paulie in the search.

They found them both outside the second balcony enjoying the breezy, fresh air. Apparently, the cat-butt hairs were contributing to their respiratory issues.

"Mamma, Papa, *buongiorno, come sta?*" Paulie asked his mother and father how they were doing.

"*Molto bene, grazie, e Lei?*" they asked.

"*Bene, grazie,*" and he hugged and kissed his mother while Melva came out onto the balcony to join them. Marcello extended his hand and kissed Melva's cheeks, his wife only nodded to her existence. Melva knew the woman was still mad about the cat hairs, and the fact that not having her son to herself.

They asked if they wanted supper for later on, Paulie told them that they had eaten a bountiful lunch and would not want to impose on their time. His mother thought nothing of it and began heading toward her domain, the kitchen, to start a hearty meal for her son.

Paulie excused himself from Marcello and Melva, he told her he had to take care of some phone calls and he'd see her shortly and reminded her to make sure she knew this was her home too now.

She kissed him, "I'll miss you, but I understand you have other things to do. Promise you'll be careful, okay. I'll go ahead and do some phone calls too, to Gerdy and Aunt Bertha. I'll make my travel arrangements for next week."

"That sounds good, *Goumada*, this way I'll have you for a whole week to show you around and show you off." His gorgeous eyes twinkled as he stared into Melva's eyes. *Does she know how much she drives me crazy?* He wished he could hold her here forever.

He wanted to take her by the coast in Vernazza; he loved it there: the church, the harbor, and the beach. He traveled there with his parents, when he was young, they would go to church and then stay near the beach and just stare out at the beautiful water. He missed his innocent childhood, wished he could live that way as an adult. *Maybe after everything settles I'll take Melva there, or another region.* He wanted to take her to so many beautiful places in Italy … he knew he would in time.

He kissed Melva between her bedroom door and the hallway and squeezed her butt, "I'll see you later, *Goumada*." He left her there in the company of his parents.

Chapter Twenty-nine

He walked around to the back of the house and then thought better of it and went to a local café; he knew that would be a good place to converse with Gino. On the way there, he still felt that presence of someone watching him, he stopped and called out to whoever it was.

"*Chi è?* Who's there?" Paulie knew the careless spy would probably be dumb enough to answer …

All of a sudden, two men jumped out, one grabbed him by the arms and the other man kicked him in the groin.

He managed to get one arm loose, pulled out his knife and drilled it into the man. The other man fled. It was so dark he couldn't make out whom the man was who got away. He didn't care to see who he had stabbed, he just took that chance to disappear and make that phone call. He knew it was someone from Castocci *brogata*.

After he caught his breath, he phoned Gino.

"*Salve*, who's this?" Gino answered the phone without suspicions.

"*Compagno*, it's me, Paulie, your line secure?" He called Gino on his cell phone, but one could never be sure.

"*Compagno! Finalmente!* Finally, you called me. Where in the hell have you been why haven't you called me earlier? What in the hell is going on there?" Gino asked impatiently to say the least.

"*Maledizione!* Damn, let me talk, *Compagno*." His patience was thin also.

"I got my nonna here, safe, but not without incidents, *capisce*?"

"*Non capisco*, what are you saying, *Compagno*?" He was confused now.

"Being 'clocked,' I guess by Castocci men? My balls are aching to kick some ass. No one screws with Nonna!"

"Damn, Gino, where in the hell did you take her?" He didn't say anything about being 'clocked' either.

"Shit, had to bring Nonna to Sicily, we tried staying with her sister near Venice, you know, had me some pretty girls lined up too, but anyway, that wouldn't have worked; Nonna would have cramped my style …"

"What the hell, someone follow you to Sicily or not?" Paulie was pissed and worried.

"Nah, I think we side-stepped 'em, you know, *Compagno*, I can be smart. I was *consigliere* for Christ's sake!"

"Yeah, well, not no more —"

"Yeah, Castocci lady-boss is gonna have us all by the damn balls if we are not careful, whatcha gonna do?" Gino went on, "hey, how's the *Goumada* doing out there with your mamma?" He snorted and knew that the transition would not be easy.

"So, where are you staying?"

"Nonna's in-laws, believe that shit – the old people still alive out here – and I ain't havin' no kinds of fun, what say I come over there?"

Paulie was glad his *Compagno's* timing was right on the money.

"*Compagno*, that's a damn good idea, when can you train it over? Oh, wait – I'm sending my *Goumada* away – next week, come then, okay. This is when I start legalizing the shipping business, I'll need you here, and advice you know?" He was happier that he had talked to his best friend.

"I'll be there, *Compagno*, hey, can you line me up somebody, you know, gorgeous," he laughed devilishly, as usual.

"I'll see who I can round up for ya. Keep in touch, come next Friday, *capisce*?"

"Yeah, okay … Nonna says *Ciao*!"

"Yeah, okay," Paulie sure didn't miss that old lady's backhand slaps.

They said their good-byes and hung up.

Paulie decided he needed a drink, nice, strong drink. While he was there, he rounded up – as promised – somebody for his *Compagno*. He was happy he had his *goumada* waiting for him and not some floozy.

After Paulie left, Melva told his parents she was not feeling well and went to her room. She slipped into her pajamas and tried to get Brinks to come into the small, cozy room so that they could cuddle. He did not go in. He had better things to do, like keep watch on the refrigerator, just in case a piece of tuna flew toward him when Ermelinda opened it.

She dialed her best friend's number, she'd try Gerdy at home, with any luck at all, she'd be there. She was so nervous and excited, because she hadn't talked to Gerdy in what seemed like forever.

Gerdy answered on the first ring, "Yeah?" Her voice revealed her sour mood.

"Gerdy, it's me, Melva. Are you all right?"

"Oh, hey girlfriend, where are you? Calling to let me in on the escapades — only give me the gory details, nothing mushy, okay go on …"

Melva giggled, "Oh Gerdy, you know we haven't gone *that* far yet."

"Well, why the hell not, damn-it did you blow the whole thing with Mr. Hot-pants already? I swear Melva, you'd think you were trying to become a nun or something, do the deed already, you're in a romantic place, right?"

Melva knew Gerdy wanted her laid and all, but she was offended that Gerdy didn't genuinely ask her how she was doing, she was thousands of miles away.

"Gerdy, you sound so 'pissy' what's the matter with you? You've been acting so mean toward me lately."

"Oh, shut-up, have not!" She mimicked a small child during a candy-tantrum.

"Well? What do you have to say for yourself? Anything at all, I'm waiting …" She thought maybe Gerdy was PMSing again, poor thing, and no one to vent toward there in Catswillow, other than her horrible boss, Earl.

Gerdy cleared her throat, "Yeah, well, it's possible I'm being a bitch about all this, I miss ya, I suppose … and the fur-wad, how's he doing?" Her voice wasn't exactly convincing, but Melva took what she could.

"Oh, your nephew is fine, he really has taken to Paulie's father, but his mother a bit tough … we'll see, I'm sure maybe she's just not use to cats."

"Yeah, maybe he's a pain in the ass," she said sternly.

"Gerdy! What the hell's the matter with you, we haven't talked in a long time, and you're being nasty, why?"

"I'm sorry, Melva, it's just work … Earl's been on my ass since I got back." Gerdy lied.

"Where did you go?" She knew Gerdy had no family to visit, not even distant relatives, well, except for her geeky, gross cousin. She shivered at the thought of that man.

"Yes, I went to see my aunt, you know my cousin's mother?" She hoped that kept Melva from going further with questions, she wasn't in the mood tonight.

"You have an aunt that's alive?" Melva was perplexed. Gerdy only had that one cousin, she never mentioned an aunt, or anyone else —all others were deceased … at least that's what Gerdy always told her.

"Silly, of course I do, she lives in Nova Scotia, and you knew this, quit being so darn crazy! Let's talk about the fine man you have got get between your legs in this millennium." Gerdy snorted, her mood had improved a bit.

She laughed too. She missed her Gerdy.

"Oh, Gerdy it's fabulous here, I wish you would come and visit me, can you? Would your boss let you? I was meaning to ask you … are you staying there at your place or with Earl like we had talked about?"

"Nah, you know me, I can take care of myself; I don't need any man protecting me from anything, you know I'll be just fine here … alone, well, with Bonbons of course." She knew how to use a gun; she found that out when they rescued Melva and Bertha.

"I know you can, but I still worry, you know like an older sister would," she wanted Gerdy to be safe above all else, and come stay with her at her aunt's mansion, "I have a great idea, why not come and stay with me at Aunt Bertha's, just outside of London, please?" She hoped Gerdy would go for it; it would be like old times.

"Sorry, girlfriend, but I gotta work. Earl's really having it rough."

"Who the hell cares, come on!" She could care less about that crazy, horrible man.

"Melva, I don't have the money or the time, so let it go, okay? Earl's trying to get other Java Jars off the ground, you'd be really impressed with him, believe me. You can always come back here."

Melva was disappointed; she felt she and her best friend were quickly drifting apart fast. She wished she knew why. Maybe it was her? But, Gerdy never had been the jealous type, ever.

"All right then, I'd better let you go, still need to call Auntie; if you change your mind —"

"I can't, bye!" Gerdy hung up the phone before Melva could say another word. She felt weird and she didn't like it, maybe Gerdy did envy her, but never had they had these issues before.

She dialed her aunt's number, Bertha answered – as always – in her Mrs. Doubtfire voice. "Hellloooo! This is Bertha!" She sang through the telephone line. Melva felt better instantly.

"Auntie, it's Melva," she suddenly remembered to use her fake English accent, just for her aunt's amusement, of course.

"Oh my dear child, it's so wonderful to hear your voice! Your auntie has been so feverishly worried about you, my dear are you all right?"

"Why, yes, Auntie —actually I'm so fabulous it's unbelievable. I have a fantastic idea, why don't I come and see you and stay for a bit, is that okay?" She couldn't wait to pack up herself and her cat, and run off to the train station.

"Melva darling, this is a wonderful idea. Come, come quickly, when can you come? Oh, my, the shopping to do, is there a wedding we need to shop for?" Her aunt giggled at the thought. She wasn't too sure if that's what she wanted for Melva ...

"No, no, calm yourself down ol' girl, but maybe in the near future, what do you think of that?" She crossed her fingers.

At that moment, Paulie peeked into her room, dropped Brinks on the floor and went over to sit by her on the bed.

She felt that 'tingle' she loved feeling.

"Auntie, I'll figure all my details out tomorrow and call you with my itinerary, okay? Shall I stay a while, or are you planning to roam around Europe?"

"Yes, come when you can, will you be bringing your Italian lover? We can chat more on him when you get here," Bertha's tone wasn't exactly thrilled at the thought; she was still having some doubts about a mobster for a nephew-in-law. But, she wanted her niece happy, that's all that mattered to her now.

Melva squirmed as Paulie's hand stroked her thigh, "Auntie, no, I'm coming alone ... oh, with Brinks of course, do you mind?"

"The little tot is welcomed, of course, so come on. Stay as long as you'd like. Do call me tomorrow." She hung the phone up after their farewells.

"Paulie what are you doing?" Paulie decided he wanted a little time with his favorite girl.

"Mamma and Papa are asleep, so no worries, *Goumada* ..."

She tried to stop him, but he was strong, but she loved it!

There was a knock on the door.

"*Maledizione!*" He cursed under his breath. "Yes?"

It was his mamma.

"*Buonanotte*, my son, is the *gatto* here in the room?" She peeked in to look about and noticed her son practically on top of Melva.

"Mamma, he's in here, so go to bed. Sorry we did not eat anything you made, but I might. Just leave it out for me, *grazie*.

Melva stood up, "*grazie*," she said awkwardly and straightened herself up a bit, as the woman stared at her disapprovingly.

Ermelinda looked around once again and noticed a furry tail half-way sticking out from under the bed, she then bid goodnight to all.

"Will she ever like me?" Melva asked, worried she may never get her approval.

"*Goumada*, do not worry, my mamma is a fair woman, she doesn't judge you at all, it just takes time. She's from many generations of traditional Italian women. Trust me, okay?" He knew how to calm her down and make her feel better.

Those eyes did magic on her body.

They decided they wanted a snack and headed toward the kitchen to feast on the talented Ermelinda's cooking.

Brinks followed them out of the room, of course. *Did someone say food?*

Chapter Thirty

The week passed very quickly. Melva packed lightly knowing that her aunt would most defiantly take her on a mega shopping spree. She hoped she wasn't exhausted by the time she got there to do that.

Brinks was finally ready to go after fighting cat claws and cat bites all the way into the carrier, he was not thrilled, he just wanted to stay there to relax and eat. He didn't take to disruptions where eating was concerned.

Nonetheless, they said their good-byes to Marcello and Ermelinda. Marcello kissed her on the cheeks, and when she hugged Ermelinda, she did not hug her back, but she thought she saw a small smile cross her face, probably because she and Brinks were leaving.

Paulie called for a cab to drop her off, but then he thought better of it and went with her to make sure no one bothered his *Goumada*. Well, the one man he stabbed couldn't, he was most likely dead and the other had probably left to give news to Castocci about the incident. He knew they were just trying to scare him into leaving all of Frankie's businesses as is, so they could jump in and take over.

Paulie dismissed the thoughts and concentrated on what he and Gino needed to do in the weeks to come, and he would have to tell his mamma, before he went anywhere else, about her brother Frankie.

Melva had a Euro Train ride up in first class, of course, for her and Brinks. Brinks had a seat all to himself of course. She hoped he wouldn't be a bad, grouchy feline all the way to London. She had told her aunt to meet her at the train station, and Bertha said that her driver would be there to pick her up, giving some excuse why she couldn't be there to greet her. Something about making Melva's room presentable for her. She didn't realize Melva would end up cleaning and changing up the room when she got there, forgetting about her niece's tendencies.

They reached the train station without incident, Paulie was happy about that; he didn't want Melva to see him blast someone's ass away. If someone had followed her to this point, then he prayed that she knew how to defend herself. His heart ached that he couldn't protect her every minute of every day. He knew that she'd be better off staying with her aunt.

"*Goumada*, call me when you get there and if someone tries anything with you, just use those shoes as weapons, *capisce*?"

They both looked down at her two-inch spiked heels she chose for the trip.

"I promise, I'll be okay you'll see. Say bye to Brinks, we both will miss you." He gave her his cell phone number; he realized she never had that until now.

"Call me whenever you want to, I'll be waiting." He kissed her passionately for all to see.

She would miss her Italian hunk.

Brinks meowed super loud for Paulie to pay attention to him, for once.

"Little guy, take care of your mamma, or else," he giggled at the recollection of the time when he thought Brinks was an actual person, a person he would have to 'whack.'

They kissed again and he gave her a nice squeeze. They boarded the first class car and waited for their train to start rolling. She was excited and sad at the same time, she wanted so much to feel Paulie beside her, but she had Brinks – besides, he was nice and warm, and furry – it would have to do for now.

She loved first class. She felt as if she were royalty. The cabin was about half full and she noticed all her fellow passengers, an old couple, a few young couples, probably on vacation, or going home and a handful of businessmen. To her they all looked very handsome; but there was one odd looking man who kept staring back at her. Dread filled within her – she noted the restroom was out right passed his seat.

When she needed to go to the restroom, for sure, she'd take Brinks with her, convincing herself that surely no one would hurt a cat-mom.

Chapter Thirty-one

"*Scusi,* Donna Castocci," the lady-boss decided she like the sound of this and made it known to her "Administration" to address her as such. Carparillini continued, "We have our secure area in *Firenze,* when do we leave?" He, who was sick of waiting for a woman to tell him what to do, he wanted control. But, he remained calm in front of the woman at the Castocci *famiglia* meeting.

"Incredible! I cannot believe my men pulled it off, why in the hell did it take forever? Am I the only one who feels this crap is taking too damn long to plan, and where in the hell is Big Bones? Must I be in the dark about everything; you men are pissing me off! I am boss, *capisce*?" The donna paced the room. The stress was getting to her and these men, whom she considered, balls for their brains, were making her even madder. She wanted Frankie's businesses tucked away for her uses, no one else's.

"What do we know about Frankie's dealings around the country, anything?"

"We have followed Paulie and his girlfriend as you instructed, but these things take time —"

The donna cut Carparillini's explanation short. "I don't give a rat's ass about who's following whom, just get me some kind of proof that I – no one else – owns these enterprises, *capisce*?"

"*Capisco,* Donna Castocci," Carparillini responded faithfully and knew that he would travel to *Firenze* and make certain the entire boss's tasks were completed.

"So, where's Big Bones, I don't see him here?" She waited patiently for any of her men to answer her. They all acted as if scared of her today. She purposely made it tough to run up and hug her.

"You will be happy to know that he's with the girl, Melva," Carparillini added.

"He's with her, what do you mean, *with*?" The donna didn't know what her cousin was up to, but hoped he grew brains and didn't screw things up for her, she'd be so pissed, she'd have to kill him this time for sure.

"He called, he's on his way to London and he'll keep an eye on the girl for us." Carparillini sat down and made himself comfortable on the couch.

They had no idea of Big Bones' intentions with Melva, Carparillini sent him to London to check out a lead he got about a pub that was a front for an underground casino. Big Bones had his own plan.

"Fine, make sure he checks in with us regularly. What else you got for me?" Castocci sat down also, across from Carparillini. She found him attractive enough for one night of passion – only. He was a little older, but she wondered if this is what she needed, to relieve some stress – a nice roll in the hay.

Carparillini cleared his throat, and gestured all the men to leave the room.

"With all respect, Donna Castocci, I think I should go to *Firenze* myself instead of staying here doing nothing; I need something to do, *capisce*?"

"*Capisco*, what did you have in mind," Castocci thought best to cross her legs at that time revealing some skin for Carparillini to see.

He saw. He liked.

"I would like to leave tomorrow, if that's all right with you, of course, Donna Castocci ..." He got up, locked the door to the room they all had met in, and went over to his lady-boss.

She wanted the same thing, and the couch would do just fine. "You can go, after you do something for me ..."

He only had to respond one way; this was by laying his hard body on top of hers.

It was a bittersweet moment when two friends hugged. Gino had finally arrived to help Paulie. The two men were more than happy to finally meet again – like old times.

"Gino, *buongiorno! Come sta?*" He patted his *Compagno* on the shoulder and then headed up to the house.

"I'm fine now, my friend, it's so very good to be here," Gino felt at home here, because he had known Paulie since his younger days chasing after Frankie everywhere Frankie would go, Paulie's parents knew this also. Therefore, he was like *famiglia* too.

"Mamma, Papa come, Gino's here!" Paulie was excited to see his friend. This meant they could head out to the hills of Vernazza, where they could deal with the shipping business.

His mamma made a bountiful lunch that consisted of veal, pork and pasta. They talked about years before and how he was such a pain in the neck for Frankie, always hanging on to him and begging to go everywhere with him. They talked about Gino's nonna and how their families would sometimes run into one another here and there across Italy, it was a nice chat.

In Italian, Gino asked Ermelinda how she felt about hearing about Frankie's death. This was a bad thing, when things were going so darn well there.

He looked at Paulie who had nearly choked on his veal, and Marcello stared at his petite wife, waiting...

He wanted to choke Gino for spilling it all, and at dinner. Ermelinda's face turned beet red, and what followed were wails of sobbing – then without warning – Ermelinda stopped as if she were a faucet someone quickly turned off.

He went over to stand next to his mother, to comfort her, "Mamma, *per favore* speak to us."

She wiped her red eyes and said, "Frankie was a bum, finish your meals, go now." She turned back toward the kitchen and began preparing a sweet treat for everyone.

The three men were perplexed at her reaction. They just nodded to one another to finish their meals and see what else the evening brought.

He wanted Gino to relax a bit, but he also wanted them to be alone to speak of plans; he wanted to head out and take to 'cleaning' along the way. The plan was to drive stopping in various places to avoid anyone following them.

After Ermelinda cleaned her kitchen, she invited her husband to join her on one of their balconies to enjoy the wonderful night air. Gino and Paulie stayed in the living room to talk of plans.

"*Compagno*, I didn't know she didn't know about her brother, Frankie, she's pissed at me, huh?" He was worried and a caring *Compagno* who hoped the woman would still make him breakfast; he missed his nonna's cooking already.

"I should kick your ass for that, but I won't, since you're here to help me," Paulie laughed and handed Gino a cigar. He didn't really like smoking around Melva, or his parents, but this was Gino, his *Compagno*.

"There is much to do?" Gino asked. He knew Paulie would pay him handsomely; after all, he helped Nonna out many times, like paying his share at the small house in Catswillow.

"We need to head out first thing tomorrow morning," Paulie noticed Gino's face showed disappointment with something that he had said. Then realized that Gino was probably thinking about food, as always, "Don't worry, *Compagno*, we'll eat breakfast first – you crazy *babbo*." They both laughed and took in a nice puff of their cigars.

"Hey, Paulie, how lucky you been gettin' with that crazy *Goumada* of yours?"

"I'm not, I told you not a good time for that, but it'll be good soon – can we get back to what I need to let you in on?" He knew Gino's mind was in the gutter at all times, then he remembered the woman he rounded up for Gino to have a good time with upon his arrival, he'd let him know this *after* they planned what they were going to do.

He told Gino they'd arrive in Monterosso al Mare by a boat to Vernazza, and there they'd seek out the man Frankie left in charge of shipping. This person wouldn't be any trouble, because this was an old man, with no ties to the mob whatsoever, this is how Frankie wanted him to appear – the less suspicions the better.

Gino would make the old man an offer he couldn't refuse, and he would proceed toward Vernazza, after the old man agreed to call in all the ships that were out of port. They would then bring those ships in, which carried drugs in the compartments, put legal products in the shipments, and made sure the authorities found the illegal drugs.

Gino agreed to do this and knew that the sooner he'd be done with the mob and connections, the better for him to find a nice woman and settle down —after all, he wasn't getting any younger.

Chapter Thirty-two

Melva arrived at the countryside mansion a little late in the evening, but nonetheless she was so happy to see the flowers in bloom and felt like a princess in her aunt's stretch limo. She absolutely loved it.

The cat squirmed a bit in his carrier, she knew he was getting a little restless in there, and thought she better let him roam around the luxurious limo. Brinks jumped out of his carrier onto the back of the leather seats. Cooped up for so long in that horrid carrier, he released his claws releasing his frustration as he popped his paws up and down.

"Oh, my goodness Brinks, Auntie Bertha will be upset at you for clawing at her leather seats, now do calm yourself." She knew her words were meaningless: Cats will do as they damn well please! They reached the main iron gates lined with an intercom and huge lions on each side of the entryway. Bertha's deceased husband figured lions looked vicious and would keep them safe. It didn't matter that he also had security roaming about to protect them.

Brinks decided to take a dive out of the limo with one swift move, as soon as the driver opened the door, "Do come and eat Brinks, you won't find anything out there but rats!" Melva hoped that latter part frightened the stubborn feline. It did not. He liked rats. Brinks tended to lick his rear before proceeding to climb the fence, and headed toward the one of several gardens Bertha's mansion owned.

"Okay, Mommy will see you at supper." She chimed and didn't really care where her cat was off to; he'd be safe around the gardens.

Her aunt heard the limo drive up and rushed out the massive wooden doors.

"My dear child, you look so thin, have you not eaten since I last saw you? I do declare you're thin as a rail, come on now —Rufus, tend to her bags, and go on." Her aunt proceeded to poke her ribs for fat.

The driver cursed at his boss under his breath, and grabbed the carrier, which smelled of kitty-cat butt, and proceeded to walk into the mansion.

Bertha bulldozed passed her many servants, using hand gestures and yelling out what each should do for her niece and her cat. Some servants dismissed her and some acknowledged Melva's presence.

Melva quickly smiled at each one, she really didn't want to be any trouble at all – but she knew that her aunt was who she was and no matter what she wanted, they would cater to her every whim regardless. She couldn't wait to go shopping!

"Now, my dear, would you like a sherry before supper, you know, to let off some of the train staleness from your body?" Bertha didn't wait for her answer she just poured the sherry.

One sip and she was a bit more relaxed. She sat back in a comfortable settee, old English furnishings draped around her. She loved the smell of the mansion. She breathed in 'old world' immediately and loved it. Nothing like luscious furniture and surroundings to make one feel so spoiled. She knew she was very lucky. She thought of her boyfriend, and what he might be doing, never once had she thought he'd stray from her ... something about him reassured her that he would not.

After their encounter, the lady-boss decided she had enough lovin' to last her a while, so she dismissed Carparillini and told him to get his nice ass out to *Firenze* at once, and then get back to her about Big Bones. She didn't really trust her new *consigliere*, her cousin Big Bones ... she knew he would screw up, she just didn't know exactly when.

Back at the mansion several days later, the ladies decided it was time for a mega shopping expedition.

First stop was a boutique located in Paris. Melva asked her aunt if this upscale boutique was the one that turned Oprah away not long ago, but Bertha had told her it was not the one. Melva didn't care, she just wanted to step where famous folk stepped.

They shopped until they couldn't shop any longer, an unusual situation for both of them. Satisfied, they were ready to head back to London's beautiful countryside. Once back, they sat in one of the many dazzling rooms with crystal chandeliers and gold leaf for one to admire. They decided that they, and Brinks, would enjoy a luscious supper in the ballroom area. They played classical music and some rock-and-roll, Bertha had stashed away, for this very special occasion with Melva.

After many hours of dancing and giggling about, Melva excused herself and Brinks to turn in. Bertha decided to linger about in her library for a mid-night read, maybe something juicy.

"Nighty-night my dear, you rest easy and tomorrow we'll ride the grounds on my horses, you'll just love Randy, he's a dream. He's popular with all the fillies." She giggled like a schoolgirl, and kissed her niece and the feline she had tucked in her arms.

"See you in the morning and thank you Auntie for this fabulous vacation."

Melva, exhausted from shopping, and Brinks headed off to dream world pretty darn quick.

It was just after 2:00 a.m. and Melva felt something weird ... she couldn't breathe. Someone had a pillow over her face! She tried to scream, but couldn't, she was petrified. And where was Brinks? *Her precious kitty, where was he?* She heard Brinks yowling and hissing, and then she heard something hit the floor hard ... she wanted to die, she knew it was her cat.

Finally, she heard someone's voice, a man's voice. She panicked, maybe one of her aunt's servants wanted to rape her.

"Listen, if you quit fighting me, bitch, I'll let you go, what's it gonna be Melva?" He knew her name.

She managed to agree to be quiet by shaking her head best she could under the pillow.

He lifted it off her head and saw the man that had kidnapped her in Catswillow! She screamed within, "What is he doing here!?" She was so terrified and confused.

He sat her up on the bed and held her wrists behind her, he was strong, and so he knew she wasn't getting away. He laid her back down on the bed and tried to kiss her,

"You remember me, don't ya baby-cakes?" He reeked of garlic and beer.

She looked at him and tried hard to recall where she'd seen him before, other than the night of the kidnapping.

"Maybe if I do you one more time, you'd remember me from that, what do ya say to that? I do remember you were not that bad, but not that great either."

She knew there was only one other man she'd been with, and that was Gerdy's geek of a cousin! Could it be? She just didn't know for sure ... she then noticed around Big Bones' face traces of scars along his hairline, could it be facial surgery.

"You do know, don't ya?" He figured by her horrific stare that she had figured out the truth.

Before she could react, Brinks jumped up from the ground and drilled his claws into the back of Big Bones' head. She was so happy her kitty was alive!

"Get him Brinks, get him!" She helped her feline out and dug her nails into his eyes, she scratched at him until she drew blood.

The door flew open and Bertha stood there shaking with a gun in her hand.

Melva flew off the bed, took the gun from her aunt, and shot once.

"Get up and get out, I never want to see the likes of you anywhere, ever, you got that," she still had the gun pointed at Big Bones, "I do this for Gerdy, you're the only family she has, go do something with your life, you big idiot."

Big Bones just nodded without another word, and left the mansion, on foot.

Bertha managed to get herself free, the stupid man had not tied the knot tight and she squeezed out of her bondage. Most of her servants were at the other end of the sprawling mansion, so they never heard any of the commotion.

The next day, without any hesitation, she decided she needed to get back to *Firenze*; she missed Paulie tremendously and wanted just to be near him again. Her aunt knew that that was best; she was in love and needed to start her own family one day. She told her aunt that she'd bring back Paulie as soon as she could, "Don't worry about anything, and just enjoy your life."

She packed up her cat and off they went back to the train station, she was tired, but wanted so much to get back home ... home in *Firenze*.

Chapter Thirty-three

Earlier that day, in the secured place that Castocci had insisted they find in *Firenze*, was Carparillini contemplating what to do next. He had tried to reach Big Bones for him to come back here, because his cousin wanted him to, but couldn't find him. The lady-boss didn't want Big Bones messing up anything, it was too late to have him any place else, so she wanted him to wait for her there.

Castocci decided she was flying out when she heard that Paulie and Gino had quickly taken Frankie's shipping business and turned it into some legit doings. This really pissed her off. She cursed at Carparillini, it didn't matter squat that she'd slept with him recently. She wanted that shipping business!

A few men had gathered there at the small meeting place and waited for their boss to arrive at any moment. They didn't know her plans, but were ready for anything she had for them to do.

Spending time cleaning up the shipping business gave Paulie and Gino time to talk about the days passed. Now looking at all they had done (they had taken that business and with no problems from the old man) they finally had themselves some cash flowing in, legal cash.

Paulie and Gino decided to contact some men, whom Paulie left in charge of the bookstore, since they were trusted, to run the shipping business, too. They wanted everyone legit in on the bookstore and the shipping business. This way Paulie and Gino could live without fear of having a contract out on them or cops sniffing around because they were suspicious about this business.

"Gino, *grazie* for the idea on what we should ship all over the world without worries," Paulie was proud of Gino, who loved to eat and knew his cuisine. His plan of shipping Italian food all around the world would make a great profit for all.

Paulie knew that this news would piss off the Castocci *brogata*. He didn't care. They were both happy and he figured he'd go out and look for that ring he told himself to purchase for his *Goumada*.

He invited Gino to go with him while his parents relaxed a bit before supper.

He picked out a pink diamond surrounded by white diamonds that cascaded all around the band, and he decided his *Goumada* deserved a nice bracelet and necklace to match it all.

When they got back, his mamma had a nice supper laid out for all her favorite men.

Castocci arrived in a wad of anger and slapped one of her men as soon as she walked into that small place.

"I'm tired, hungry and tired," she exclaimed to all her men. "We get Paulie tonight and we get him good. Lead the way Carparillini." She knew that he had found out where Paulie's parents lived.

Castocci, Carparillini and two other crewmembers headed over to the Palazollo residence. It was dark out, but they found the house in no time. The lights were dim in the house, but she could see movement.

"You two go around the back, I'm climbing the balcony." She had leather pants and boots on, and she moved like a cat. She was serious!

Carparillini followed his boss up the balcony.

Paulie's mamma and papa had already gone to bed when he heard Gino snoring at the other end of the room. He was beat and decided to get a tiny snack before heading down to his room. Gino would sleep there; he didn't care at this time. Just as he was about to open the refrigerator, two men jumped on him and tackled him to the floor.

They knocked him out, last he remembered was seeing Melva's friend, the one with the wild hair and attitude.

"Hey, wake up, come on, we don't have all damn night," she tapped Paulie on the head. "Carparillini, make sure the other one's no problem," she pointed to where Gino was, lying on the floor, face down, but not dead.

"What the hell lady – what are you doing here in my damn house?" Paulie was pissed and in shock.

"Welcome to Gerdy-world," her sinister laugh told him this was no joke.

"All will be all right if you hand over the shipping business to me, right now, *capisce*?" She waited, stared at him with blazing, evil eyes.

He had no idea this was Castocci, who else? She was a woman, and that's what the word out there was, that the new boss was a woman. But, this was Melva's friend from her childhood? He could not comprehend; it was too farfetched, even for the mob.

Castocci could see he had conflictions within. "Are you ready then to die, no big deal for me, Melva will never find out anyway ... she knows me as Gerdy Drake, not Castocci, she'd never believe you anyway, so out with it before I put this bullet in your Italian head."

What she didn't know was that he and Gino managed to funnel millions through a Swiss bank under Brinks' name. In a million years, even a mob boss would never know.

At first, they stopped all the ships from sailing by telling the captains that they were being 'clocked' and to get out before the mob came in and made threats against their families. Frankie never made threats to these men, because he knew they all needed the money, and besides they had known Frankie for years and trusted his word. After the ships were free from those men, Paulie and Gino moved the other men from Catswillow in to take over.

He spit out some blood that was gathering in his mouth, right at her face, "You can have it all and I don't give a damn what you do, hear me."

She had thought she won the battle with him. "See Carparillini, he can come to reason and do the right thing ... for Melva, right?" She looked at him and then slapped him. "I'm done with you, but just one thing before we go from here ... tell my best friend you heard I died in a car accident or make up something, I don't want her in my life — it's just not gonna work, *capisce*?" Her heart, for a moment, sank. She then remembered who she was and thought it better that it ended this way.

She came and went without another person hurt and Big Bones would leave Melva alone per her request. This wasn't the first time she'd save his ass.

Paulie didn't know if she would come after him after she found out about her new business being legit, and with hardly any money coming in at all, but he felt, for some odd reason that she wouldn't come after Melva or him for that matter.

They were safe.

When Melva arrived late that night, she walked into a bit of a ruckus. "What's going on here, Paulie?" She noticed the house turned upside down. She cringed at the mess and wanted Ermelinda to know she'd like to help clean up the whole mess. Looked as if someone broke in, but she didn't know for sure.

Paulie went over to her and hugged her hard, "Want to help Mamma clean up a bit?" He knew she did. He managed a smile, but was terribly bothered about what he found out: Gerdy, her best friend, the Castocci *famiglia* boss. He couldn't get this whole bizarre situation about Gerdy out of his mind, but he knew he had to. *Just try to forget, best for all.* Paulie thought it best that they move on with their lives – together, which he knew would be an adventure in itself.

Chapter Thirty-four

A month or so past without incident, he thanked the heavens above, and he and Melva began to officially date. This brought happiness into a situation that had been filled with all the kidnappings, and the dreaded news that he'd given Melva about Gerdy.

At first, she was in shock and thought she would die; he let her alone for a week or so to grasp her emotions on losing her best friend. He knew otherwise, and so did Gino. His parents never knew what went down at their house, just that when they woke up, as Melva came back from London, that someone had broken in looking for jewels, as this is what he and Gino had told them.

Melva contemplated whether to go back to Catswillow, or stay here in paradise she chose the latter. There was nothing in Catswillow, well except for Lomechick, but she knew that that woman would still be upset about her waking her up late at night a long time ago. She thought best to sell her condo and have the Mercedes that Aunt Bertha had bought her, shipped over. Paulie took care of all the details.

Gino bought Nonna a vineyard outside Tuscany and made sure that she made up a room just for him when he came to visit her.

Bertha came over to console her only niece after Melva called frantically that Gerdy had died in a car accident. She ended up staying a spell, she rather liked the mundane life Paulie's parents lead in *Firenze*. She and Gino hit it off fabulously so much so, that they began their own courtship. This became something of an odd affair, but who cared, they were happy —after all that's what really mattered in a relationship.

Paulie proposed to Melva on a gorgeous spring day. The sunflowers were the most beautiful, and the surrounding sights and sounds were so happy. He thought it best to take her and Brinks too, to the Almafi coast, just south of Naples.

She fell in love with her ring, and the Almafi coast. Paulie, she knew she loved, from the first moment she saw him.

His mamma even sent her a charm with Saint Francis of Assisi to Brinks, and told them to go to the nearest church on Sunday to see the Father there – it was Blessings of the Animals – and Brinks should be first in line since he needed it most.

Gino called him and said that he and Bertha would be arriving in style, to join the two lovebirds.

She was so happy she thought she would burst, but Paulie kept reminding her that she deserved all the happiness the world had to offer her. She felt that she did, too.

She knew Brinks was happy also, this cat had a whole ocean of fish to boot! The cat even won the heart of Ermelinda – that was not an easy feat to accomplish in such a short time. He was a special soul, to her most of all.

Her toes curled in the moment of extreme passion.

He felt something cold – and furry – on his butt.

Brinks.

"What the f—!" He turned his head to see Brinks on his buttocks.

She reached for Paulie, "Don't stop!"

"Damn cat —Melva is he going to do this all the time?"

Brinks didn't move an inch. He rather liked the nice, soft, smooth area his paw had found.

She looked passed Paulie's shoulder, "Um, well, I don't know … he's never done this before." Her heavy breathing continued. "Oh, just ignore him. He won't do anything but sit there, really, he doesn't bother *me*."

He ignored the cat and continued to please *his* female.

www.ingramcontent.com/pod-product-compliance
Lightning Source LLC
Chambersburg PA
CBHW071958150726
47999CB00001B/482